Fenella Fang and the Great Escape

Ritchie Perry

Illustrated by Jean Baylis

Hutchinson

Hutchinson
London Melbourne Auckland Johannesburg

Copyright © Text Richie Perry 1987
Copyright © Illustrations Jean Baylis 1987

All rights reserved

First published in 1987 by Hutchinson Children's Books
An imprint of Century Hutchinson Ltd
Brookmount House, 62–65 Chandos Place, Covent Garden,
London WC2N 4NW

Century Hutchinson Publishing Group (Australia) Pty Ltd
16–22 Church Street, Hawthorn, Melbourne, Victoria 3122

Century Hutchinson Group (NZ) Ltd
32–34 View Road, PO Box 40-086, Glenfield, Auckland 10

Century Hutchinson (SA) Pty Ltd
PO Box 337, Bergvlei 2012, South Africa

Set in Baskerville by BookEns, Saffron Walden, Essex
Printed and bound in Great Britain by Anchor Brendon Ltd,
Tiptree, Essex

British Library Cataloguing in Publication Data
Perry, Ritchie
Fenella Fang and the great escape
I. Title
823'.914[J]   PZ7

ISBN 0-09-171910-0

One

Fenella Fang was late and it was all Gertrude Guzzle's fault. When she had arranged the Humaneen party for a few of her closest friends, Fenella had known some of the younger vampires would turn up at the crypt as well, playing pick or eat in their hideous human masks. She hadn't expected Gertrude to arrive and then invite herself in to the party. Although Gertrude had eaten all the toad's liver sandwiches and most of the frog's-eye pasties, Fenella didn't mind this too much. She had prepared more than enough food and, even with Gertrude there, there was plenty for the guests to eat. No, Gertrude's main trouble was that she was in love with the sound of her own voice. Once she had started talking it was almost impossible to make her stop. As Melissa Munch had whispered in Fenella's ear, it was a good thing vampires never died. Otherwise Gertrude would certainly have bored them all to death.

As morning had approached, the other guests came up to Fenella one by one and thanked her for a lovely night before they flew off. Not Gertrude Guzzle, though. Even after everybody else had left, she stayed on and on . . . and on and on and on. In the end, Fenella had had enough.

'It's been very nice seeing you again, Gertrude,' she said, 'but I'm afraid you really must fly off now. It's nearly daylight and I still have all the clearing up to do.'

'You're behind the times, Fenella dear.' Gertrude hadn't moved from her perch near the roof of the crypt. 'You'll never guess what I've just had fitted to my coffin.'

'No, I probably won't.'

So many gadgets had been installed in Gertrude's coffin it was a wonder she could still squeeze inside.

'It's a dishwasher, dear, and it's absolutely marvellous.'

Despite all Fenella's efforts to get rid of her, it was another thirty snaps* before Gertrude had finished explaining the wonders of the new machine. Fenella was usually a kindly soul but, by the time her uninvited guest had eventually departed, she was hoping the dishwasher would spring a leak while its owner was in her coffin. *Then* Gertrude could find out how good she was at talking underwater. Thanks to her, the sun was already climbing into the sky outside before

*1 snap = 1 human minute

6

Fenella had climbed wearily into her coffin. It was hardly surprising she had overslept.

Most nights this wouldn't have mattered too much, but Fenella was supposed to be flying up to Blood Castle to visit her uncle. Uncle Samuel was probably the most famous of all the vampires. However much humans might talk about Fenella's other uncle, Drac, among vampires themselves Samuel Suck was far better known. For a start, at two thousand three hundred and twenty-two, he was the oldest of them all by far, and the only one without any teeth. However, his greatest claim to fame was as an inventor and this was why Fenella had been invited over. Samuel wanted his favourite niece to be the first to see his latest invention. And although she had no idea what this might be, Fenella certainly didn't want to keep her uncle waiting.

The trouble was, the more Fenella hurried, the more time she seemed to waste. First of all she smudged her lipstick and had to do it all over again. Then there was the accident with the clothes drawer: for the past few nights it had been sticking in the damp weather and it needed a really sharp tug to free it. Tonight, though, the drawer decided not to stick at all. When Fenella pulled at it, the drawer came shooting out of the coffin so suddenly that Fenella sat down with a bump while her shrouds went shooting all over the crypt floor.

By the time she was finally ready, Fenella was in such a hurry she completely forgot the present she had for her uncle. She had actually left the crypt before she remembered and she had to fly back down to collect it. 'Creaking coffin lids,' she muttered to herself. 'This definitely isn't going to be my night.'

Fenella was absolutely right because there was worse to come. SAPS* are something all vampires learn about from the moment they first start to fly. In fact, they were one of Samuel Suck's earliest and most successful inventions. Apart from when they have a hole in them, pockets are no problem for humans; unless they are stupid enough to try walking on their hands or standing on their heads, their pockets always hang downwards and whatever is in them can't possibly fall out. For a vampire, though, it is very different. For a vampire swooping around the night sky, nothing in an ordinary pocket is safe and, as vampires come down headfirst until almost on the ground, landings are especially awkward. In the early nights, before the invention of SAPS, every vampire was likely to land in a hail of talon-trimmers, beauty warts, tooth sharpeners and anything else they happened to have in their pockets. Then, of course, after they had safely landed, everything had to be picked up again. Apart from wasting an awful lot

* SAPS = Safety Pockets

8

of time, this could lead to unpleasant accidents. Charlie Chomp had nearly had his ear cut off by a pair of scissors he was carrying and Fu Chew, the Chinese vampire, had ended up with a chopstick stuck up his nose.

Fortunately, the invention of SAPS had changed all this. Now every vampire carefully closes his Vampcro pocket seals before a flight and takes care not to open them again until safely back on the ground. It was something Fenella herself had done thousands of times, something which was almost as automatic as closing her coffin lid before going to sleep.

Tonight, though, was different. Fenella was in so much of a hurry she simply scooped Uncle Samuel's present into a pocket before she flew off again. When she realized her mistake a few snaps later, it was already too late. The neatly-wrapped package had slipped out of the pocket and was plummeting earthwards through the dark night air. At the speed Fenella was flying, there was no question of catching it before it reached the ground. The best she could do was swoop round in a great circle and watch carefully to see where it landed. Even here she was unlucky. There were plenty of open fields for the package to fall into, but it had to land slap-bang in the middle of the only wood in sight.

'Dracula's teeth,' Fenella cursed. 'This really is too much.'

Still muttering under her breath, she flew down towards the wood. Now she would be later than ever.

There weren't very many humans who had actually met a vampire. Bert Bungle had, though, and the experience had been enough to change his entire life. There he had been, quietly going about his business as a burglar, when this great bat had appeared out of nowhere to scare the living daylights out of him with its burning red eyes and flashing white teeth. This was the night Bert had given up being a burglar for ever. In fact, for some time afterwards he didn't even dare to leave the house after dark unless Mrs Bungle went with him to hold his hand. As this interfered with her bingo, it wasn't long before Mrs Bungle had packed him off to see the doctor.

'Are you sure it was a vampire you saw, Mr Bungle?' the doctor had asked.

'Of course I am. It was called Fenella. And there was a little girl with it called Heinz Beans.'

'I see, Mr Bungle,' said the doctor. The poor fellow is stark, raving bonkers, he thought to himself. He's completely round the twist.

'The trouble is,' Bert went on, 'I'm scared of the dark now. I keep thinking the vampire is after me again. What can I do?'

'That's easy, Mr Bungle.' The doctor was beginning to think he would be scared to go out after dark, too, if he knew there were nutcases like Bert wandering around in it. 'It's simply a matter of getting used to the dark again. I suggest you try walking around with your eyes closed during the daytime; after a while you won't find the dark nearly so bad.'

The doctor had been right. Although Bert was always banging his nose against lampposts or falling down open manholes, keeping his eyes closed during the day did make the night-time much less frightening. Unfortunately, it did nothing to help Bert go back to being a burglar. He had been breaking into a house when the vampire had appeared and this was something Bert couldn't forget.

'Well, you'll have to do something, Bert,' Mrs Bungle told him at last. 'We need the money. Why don't you get yourself a job?'

'Get myself a job?' Bert could hardly believe his ears. 'None of us Bungles have ever worked. Besides, how can I get myself a job if I have to keep my eyes closed all day?'

'What are you going to do then? – sit around here and starve?'

'We're going to move to the country, that's what,' Bert told her. 'I'm going to be a poacher. I'll go out at night and catch rabbits and pheasants and things. We'll have plenty to eat and I can sell the rest to the butcher's.'

Mrs Bungle laughed so much she gave herself a

stitch in the side. 'Don't be so daft, Bert Bungle,' she said when she had calmed down. 'You've never seen a rabbit or a pheasant in your life. Besides, you're lucky if you can catch a cold, let alone a wild animal. You wouldn't have the slightest idea how to do it.'

'That's where you're wrong, Clever Clogs. All I have to do is creep up on them in the dark and boink them with a club.'

'Creep up on them?' Mrs Bungle had started laughing again. 'Why, you're so clumsy you can't cross the room without tripping over your own feet.'

I'll show the silly old haddock, Bert had thought to himself. But Mrs Bungle had been right: although they had moved into the country and Bert had been out poaching every night for three weeks, he still hadn't caught anything. The trouble was, it was so dark in the woods he could hardly see his hand in front of his face, let alone any animals. So far, Bert had crept up on lots of bushes and boinked them with his club, along with several tree stumps and one old petrol can somebody had left lying around, but he hadn't been near a rabbit or pheasant.

'Tonight's the night, though,' Bert said to him-self as he crouched among the trees of the small wood. 'This is the night when my luck changes.'

A couple of minutes later, when he heard a rustling in the undergrowth to his right, Bert was certain he had been correct. Although it sounded more like something falling than the movement of an animal, there was no wind to blow anything from the trees.

'It must have been a pheasant laying an egg,' Bert thought. 'It was probably standing up when it did it.'

For a while nothing much happened. There were no more noises and it was too dark for Bert to distinguish anything apart from the vague outline of the trees. Then Bert's patience was suddenly rewarded: there was a flapping of wings and he saw the dim shape of a bird settling to the ground not very far in front of him. Even in the darkness, Bert could see that it was a large bird. In fact, it was a *very* large bird indeed.

Cor blimey, he thought. It's more like a flying elephant than a bird. Pheasants didn't look that big in the picture I saw. Not that this mattered. Although Bert had never seen a real, live pheasant before, he did know they weren't dangerous and the bigger the bird, the more meat he would have to sell.

Gripping his club in both hands, Bert began to creep towards the unsuspecting pheasant, careful not to make a sound. The closer he came to the bird, the bigger it seemed to grow. It was poking around in the undergrowth as though it was looking for something. It's trying to find its egg, Bert decided.

13

He was right behind the pheasant now and he could see just how enormous it was. It would obviously need a really hard boink to deal with this one! Lifting his club above his head, Bert rose up on his toes before hitting the pheasant as hard as he could.

'Ouch,' the pheasant said. 'That hurt.'

Bert hadn't realized that pheasants could talk but he wasn't about to stop now. Raising his club again, he hit the pheasant even harder.

'Ouch,' the pheasant repeated.

A second later, Bert realized his mistake. Fenella had been crouched down, looking for Uncle Samuel's present, but now she stood up, rising to her full height so that she towered above the terrified Bert Bungle. She also turned round and for the first time Bert saw her red eyes which glowed like burning embers. Dark as it was, he could also see the great, white teeth which filled her mouth. It was the same hideous vampire Bert had met once before, and he had just boinked her with his club.

'What do you think you're doing, you horrible little human?' Fenella hissed angrily, rubbing her head.

Bert couldn't answer any more than he could run; his entire body seemed to have turned to jelly. When Fenella took the club away from him, he simply stood there with his mouth hanging wide open.

'Let's see how you like it,' she said.

Fenella used the club to give Bert a gentle tap on the head. At least, for a vampire it was gentle; for a human it was very hard indeed and Bert suddenly recovered his voice. 'Ooowww,' he yelled. 'Oooooowwwwww. You've cracked my cranium.'

'It serves you right,' Fenella hissed, angrily. 'Now you know what it feels like.'

She would have liked to tap Bert's head a few more times, just to teach him a proper lesson, but she had noticed something. Vampires can see very well in the dark and although all humans looked more or less the same to Fenella, there was something familiar about this man. She reached out and lifted Bert from the ground as though he was a baby, holding him up so she could examine him more closely. Bert was sure his last moment must have come.

'N-n-n-ice v-v-v-ampire,' he stuttered. 'P-p-p-lease d-d-d-on't b-b-ite m-m-m-e a-a-a-nd and s-s-suck m-m-y bl-bl-bl-ood.'

'Don't be so silly.'

The very thought made Fenella feel quite ill. No vampire would ever want to drink dirty, warm human blood when they could have a nice glass of iced HBS*. Humans really did have the strangest ideas about vampires.

'Haven't I met you somewhere before?' she asked.

Bert shook his head so hard his cheeks wobbled and his ears flapped. Although Fenella didn't really believe him, she didn't have time to waste on him; she was becoming later by the moment.

'Well, you'd better make sure I don't ever meet you again,' she hissed.

For one wonderful moment Bert thought she was about to set him free, but he was wrong. With a couple of flaps from her powerful wings, Fenella soared into the air, taking Bert with her.

'Put me down, you monster,' he screeched. 'Us poachers aren't supposed to fly.'

*HBS = Human Blood Substitute

'They aren't supposed to hit vampires on the head either,' Fenella told him. 'Are you sure you want me to let you go?'

'Ye . . . . I mean no.' Bert had just realized how high up they were.

'I thought you might change your mind. Now, you just stay here.' Fenella had hooked his belt on to a branch near the top of a tall oak tree. 'That should keep you out of trouble.'

Before Bert had a chance to say anything, Fenella had vanished down into the darkness. She still had Uncle Samuel's present to find.

Samuel Suck's servant, Igor, wasn't very good-looking. In fact, if there had ever been a competition to find the ugliest man in the world, Igor would probably have easily won it. He looked like somebody who had been getting ready for a part in a horror film and then forgotten to remove any of the make-up. Chickens didn't lay any more eggs after they had seen him, other humans had nightmares, and even Igor himself didn't look in mirrors because it was too frightening. He was absolutely hideous.

For a start, his bald head was covered with warts and a greenish mould which grew because he never, ever washed. This was his parents' fault. If you were made to wear a brown paper bag over your head all the time you were young, you wouldn't be able to wash either. However, not using soap or water did mean that Igor smelled rather. To be honest, he stank something rotten and most people tried not to breathe in too much when Igor was near them. The only people who were grateful for his dreadful pong were those living in the village near Blood Castle. Provided they didn't have bad colds, they always knew when Igor was coming and this gave them plenty of time to put on their blindfolds so they didn't have to look at him.

Igor's entire body looked as though it had been made out of spare parts by somebody who was very drunk at the time. His eyes, nose and mouth were squeezed to one side of his head while on the other there was a single, huge ear. His arms and legs were all different sizes so Igor found it very difficult to walk in a straight line or use a knife and fork properly. Not that Igor ever bothered with a knife and fork; he preferred to eat with his hands, which was really disgusting when it was something like mashed potato or custard. A lot of the food usually ended up on Igor's clothes, and as these were never washed or changed, they didn't smell too good either.

On this particular night, standing high on the castle battlements, Igor looked even more hideous than usual. Apart from all the other things which were wrong with him, he had a huge hump on his back. This was caused by Samuel Suck's latest invention, which was strapped firmly to his shoulders. It was also the reason Igor was so unhappy. 'Why does it have to be me, Master?' he wailed, staring nervously at the ground far below.

'It's a reward for your years of faithful service, Igor,' Samuel told him with a smile. 'Just think of the honour. You'll be the very first to test one of my most important inventions.'

'But I don't want the honour, Master. It might kill me.'

'Poppycock, Igor. Absolute balderdash. I've invented thousands of things and no vampire has ever been killed yet.'

'But nothing can kill a vampire, Master. I'm a *human*.'

'All right then, when have you ever known one of my inventions to fail?'

'There was COD, Master.'

'Stuff and nonsense. That didn't fail. It just worked a little bit too well.'

The Coffin Opening Device had been one of Samuel's recent experiments. It was supposed to open the coffin lid automatically when night fell but it hadn't been a great success. When Samuel had fitted it to his coffin, the lid had been opening and closing all day long, every time a cloud passed in front of the sun. Poor Samuel hadn't had a wink of sleep and he had nearly had a nasty accident when the lid started closing while he was climbing out.

'What about LOB then, Master. I haven't seen you use that much.'

The Lift-Off Belt had been rocket powered. Worn around the waist, it was intended for use in cramped spaces where there wasn't room for the vampire to unfurl his wings. The rockets would shoot him up into the air until he was high enough to fly properly. Unfortunately, when Samuel had tested it, the rockets had set fire to his feet and he had to make an emergency landing in a nearby pond to put out the flames. It had been several weeks before Samuel had been able to walk without a limp.

Luckily, Samuel was saved the need to answer. His vampire eyes had just spotted a fast-moving dark speck approaching Blood Castle. 'Ah, there's Fenella at last,' he said. 'I was beginning to think she wasn't coming.'

It was only a few seconds before a rather breathless Fenella joined them on the battlements. She had been flying at top speed to make up for lost time. 'I'm sorry I'm so late,' she said once she had landed. 'I'm afraid I've had one of those nights.'

'Not to worry, dear,' Samuel told her, nuzzling her neck affectionately. 'You're here and that's the main thing. We'll begin the experiment at once. I've had a hard job stopping young Igor here from trying out my invention before you arrived.'

'Oh no he hasn't, Mistress. I don't want to do it at all.'

'Pay no attention to him, Fenella; Igor is just being modest. He was keen to have a go from the moment I first mentioned it to him.'

'The master tricked me, Mistress.' Now Igor was angry as well as frightened. 'He asked me if I wanted to try a SALAD and I thought it was something to eat. I didn't know it was a Safety Landing Device.'

'A Safety Landing Device, Uncle?' Like Samuel, Fenella was paying no attention to Igor; she was used to his moods. 'That sounds interesting.'

'It is, Fenella, it is. The SALAD is for vampires who get cramp in their wings while they're flying or have an accident. Humans have something like it for when they're flying in those noisy machines of theirs. They call it a parakeet or something silly.'

'How does your invention work?' Fenella asked.

'It's quite simple, dear,' Samuel said. 'When you're in trouble, you pull a handle, the SALAD opens up above you and you float gently down to the ground. I'm really excited about it.'

'I'm not,' said Igor, who was scared stiff. 'I think one of you two should test it first. Both of you can fly if anything goes wrong.'

'But that's the whole point, Igor,' Samuel explained. 'It wouldn't be a proper test if *we* tried it out. You can't fly at all, so when you land safely we know the SALAD has worked.'

'You're missing my point, Master. What happens if I don't land safely?'

'Don't be such a spoilsport,' Fenella told him. 'You know Uncle Samuel would never let you test the SALAD unless he knew it would work.'

'That's right, Igor. It really couldn't be simpler. When we throw you off the battlements, all you have to do is count up to three and pull the handle. Come on, Fenella; you take his other arm.'

'But, Master . . . .'

Igor didn't have a chance to say any more because Fenella and Samuel had taken an arm apiece and hoisted him up on to the wall. After this, Igor was too busy stopping himself from falling to speak. Balancing wasn't at all easy if your legs were different lengths.

'Now remember, Igor. Count up to three and then pull the handle.'

'But, Master, I can't— Hhheeelllppp!'

Samuel had given his servant a push in the back and Igor was suddenly tumbling downwards. Both Fenella and her uncle leaned out over the battlements to watch. Nothing much was happening except that Igor was hurtling towards the moat at tremendous speed.

'Shouldn't Igor have pulled the handle by now, Uncle?'

'He is leaving it rather late,' Samuel agreed anxiously.

Splash! Igor disappeared into the greasy water of the moat. A few seconds later he reappeared with a water lily draped behind his ear and a startled duck perched on his bald head. 'But, Master . . . glub, glub . . . I can't . . . glub, glub . . . count up . . . glub, glub . . . to three,' Igor screamed. 'And I can't . . . glub, glub . . . swim either.'

He was just sinking beneath the surface of the water when Fenella swooped down to pull him from the moat.

Two

There were no further tests of the SALAD that night. It had to be hung up to dry as did Igor, who had drunk quite a lot of water from the moat before he was rescued. He had also swallowed several tadpoles and a stickleback, but it wasn't long before he was himself again. In fact, he insisted on serving Fenella her meal in the Great Hall. Igor always prepared something special when he knew she was coming and tonight he had made her some maggot sandwiches. They were one of her favourites.

'You should try one, Uncle,' she said. 'They're absolutely delicious.'

'I only wish I could,' Samuel answered gloomily. Ever since he had lost his teeth, Samuel had had great difficulty eating. Apart from HBS and soft foods like toad's brain porridge, there wasn't much he could manage.

'Perhaps you can,' Fenella said. 'I've brought you a present.'

She handed her uncle the package which she

had eventually found in the wood. Samuel Suck eagerly opened it and for a moment he simply stared at what was inside. 'They're wonderful, dear,' he said at last, 'just what I wanted. What are they exactly?'

'What do they look like, Uncle?'

'Well, they look like teeth but they're not inside a mouth.' Samuel was sounding puzzled.

'That's just what they are. They're my own first invention and they should help you eat properly again. They're False Replacement Teeth.'

'You could call from FART for short, Mistress,' said Igor, dribbling with excitement.

'Don't be so disgusting.' Samuel leaned out of his chair to cuff Igor around the ear before he turned back to his niece. 'How do they work, Fenella? Do I hold some of the teeth in each hand and mash the food between them?'

'Oh no, Uncle. They fit inside your mouth like ordinary teeth – you'll be able to eat like a proper vampire again.'

It took Samuel a while to get them fitted. The first time he tried they were upside down and the fangs stuck up his nostrils. However, after Fenella had shown him how to do it he soon had them in place and, with the new teeth in his mouth Samuel looked very different. They were on the large side and the old vampire suddenly looked rather frightening. Even Igor, who had been working with vampires all his life, drew back slightly.

25

'You don't half look fierce, Master,' he said nervously.

Samuel didn't pay any attention. He had picked up one of the maggot sandwiches and cautiously he held it up to his mouth. When he bit down on it, the new teeth went through the sandwich like a knife through butter.

'You'll have to be careful of your fingers, Master,' Igor told him. 'Otherwise you might bite them off.'

The old vampire still wasn't paying any attention. He could chew as well with the new teeth and he was shoving maggot sandwiches into his mouth as fast as he could. It was forty-three years since he had last enjoyed a real meal and he was making up for lost time. As the teeth were made of metal they clanged a bit as he ate and there was the odd spark, but this didn't bother Samuel at all. He didn't stop munching until the last of the sandwiches had gone. Then he sat back in his chair with a wide, satisfied smile on his face.

'What do you think of them, Uncle?' Fenella asked.

'Ay stink stair obsholutily merhulouse,' he answered contentedly.

'What did you say?' Fenella hadn't been able to understand a word.

'Ay shed ay stink stair obsholutily merhulouse.'

'I think the master is inventing again, Mistress,' Igor said. 'He's made up a new language.'

'Dent bay sue sally,' Samuel said irritably. 'Ay jam stalking pearlifically hormonely.'

Fenella and Igor looked at each other in amazement, wondering what could have happened. Then the answer suddenly occurred to Fenella. 'It's the new teeth, Uncle. They're stopping you from talking properly.'

Fenella explained that the teeth might be fine for eating but they prevented anybody from understanding what Samuel was saying. Although Fenella was rather upset by this, Samuel Suck was still delighted by her present. As he said, once he had removed them from his mouth, teeth were only important when you were eating. For the rest of the time they just took up a lot of space. He was quite happy to put them in at mealtimes and remove them again afterwards.

'In fact,' he said, 'I think I'll pop them back in now and test them some more. Igor, you run off to the kitchen and prepare some more sandwiches. You'd better make plenty because I'm sure Fenella will want some too.'

'I don't know, Uncle,' said Fenella sounding doubtful. 'It's getting late. I ought to be flying back home.'

'Stuff and nonsense, Fenella. Igor will prepare the spare coffin for you after he's made the sandwiches. Now I have my new teeth I feel like celebrating, and I can't do that on my own.'

Although Fenella agreed to stay and enjoyed

herself almost as much as her uncle, neither of them would have been at all cheerful if they had known what lay in store for them. At that very moment, a large lorry was heading towards Blood Castle and the driver was bringing nothing but trouble with him.

Spiro Pasta was one of the richest men in the world and he was also one of the nastiest. Making money was the only thing which interested him and he didn't care how he did it. For example, when he was a young boy, Spiro used to offer to help blind people across busy roads; then he would threaten to leave them stuck in the middle unless they gave him all their money. Even worse, one night he put an alarm clock inside his bed-ridden grandmother's hot-water bottle and pre-tended the ticking was a bomb. And he wouldn't take the hot-water bottle out of her bed until she gave him all of her pension. When he went into a shop, Spiro never, ever paid for anything. In fact, the shops used to pay him: he would ask for a penny sweet and pay for it with a ten-pound note attached to a piece of elastic. Not only did he get nine pounds and ninety-nine pence in change but the ten-pound note always shot back into his pocket as well. Nor was this all: he had a special magnet which stopped slot machines just where he wanted and, of course, he always took money from other children who were smaller and younger than him. If they were silly enough not to pay Spiro would send his friends, the Lasagna brothers, after them and they were even nastier than Spiro himself.

By the time he left school, Spiro already had enough money to open his own restaurant and it was here he made his fortune. He did it with his special slippery spaghetti, which was cooked in Vaseline and slid right off the customers' forks. As the spaghetti was always left on the plate, it could be sold hundreds of times to hundreds of different customers. Some of the customers did try to pick the spaghetti up with their fingers instead of using forks, but they would be thrown straight out of the restaurant for having bad manners. Of course, this was probably very lucky for the customers: spaghetti cooked in Vaseline tastes absolutely horrid.

It wasn't very long before Spiro Pasta had lots of restaurants, all of them selling slippery spaghetti. Spiro was a millionaire but this wasn't enough for him; he grew richer and richer and nastier and nastier. Even though he was so rich, guests at his mansion were never given anything to eat except dry bread and slippery spaghetti. Worse still, every toilet in the mansion was fitted with a coin machine and Spiro had the only key. Guests had to pay a pound every time they wanted to go to the lavatory and then found they had to pay another pound before they could get out. Most of Spiro's

visitors spent a lot of time sitting with their legs crossed, feeling hungry.

Although Spiro didn't like animals and was almost as cruel to them as he was to people, there was a zoo in the grounds of his mansion. He charged admission so it was simply another way of making money. There were aardvarks and aye-ayes, baboons and buzzards, caymans and coyotes, all through the alphabet to zebras and zorillas. (A zorilla is an African polecat which looks rather like a skunk. When it is frightened or upset it can give off a truly horrible pong, just like a skunk. This was why it was the only one of the small animals in the zoo which Spiro never poked with his steel-tipped walking stick. He had already stopped poking the larger animals after one of the gorillas had pulled the walking stick through the bars of his cage and started poking Spiro back. Incidentally, Spiro didn't need the stick to help him walk properly. He only used it for poking the animals and tripping up old ladies who were carrying a lot of shopping. Occasionally he also used it to crack Laszlo Lasagne on the shins, but this wasn't much fun – Laszlo had such a small brain, he didn't realize he had been hurt until a day or two afterwards.)

Spiro was very proud of his zoo, not only because it made him a lot of money but because people came from all over the world to see it. However, to make it complete (and so that he could double admission charges) he would have liked to own one animal which wasn't in any other collection anywhere in the world. 'There must be an animal somewhere that nobody else has,' Spiro said. We need something really special. Something no other zoo can possibly have. What we need is a vampire.'

'A vampire,' Laszlo said, scratching his head. 'What do we want with somebody who gives people out at cricket.'

'Don't be so stupid, Laszlo,' Spiro and Luigi

said together. 'That's an umpire.'

People were always telling Laszlo he was stupid and this was when they were being kind. 'I thought you only found vampires in films and books, Boss.'

'I hope not for the sake of you and your idiotic brother.' Spiro was smiling an evil smile. 'It's your job to find a vampire for me.'

Although Luigi pleaded and pleaded with him Spiro refused to change his mind. He had set his heart on his very own vampire and it was up to the Lasagnas to find him one.

The problem they had was knowing where to begin. First of all Luigi tried putting an advertisement in the local newspaper but, to his disappointment, not a single vampire answered it. Next he tried the local library where he stole a book about vampires. (Of course, he could have borrowed the book for free but both brothers preferred to steal things when they could.) Luigi read the book through from cover to cover, which was very hard work as he wasn't much brighter than his brother. However, when he had finished the book, Luigi had the answer to the problem.

'It's pretty easy when you're an expert on vampires,' he said, closing the book with a bang. 'All vampires leave luminous footprints which glow in the dark and all of them live in big nests at the top of oak trees.'

'Luminous footprints?' Laszlo repeated. 'Big nests in oak trees?' Daft as he was, this sounded very strange to him.

'That's what it says in *Vincent the Vampire Goes to Mars*,' Luigi told him. 'There's even a picture to prove it. Look, there are the glowing footprints and the nest is up there.'

'Is that Vincent?' Laszlo asked. He liked books with pretty pictures.

'That's right.'

For the next few weeks the Lasagna brothers spent all their days looking up into oak trees for big nests and their nights looking down at forest floors for luminous footprints. If it hadn't been for Laszlo, they might have gone on for ever without finding anything. No vampire has ever lived in a nest in an oak tree, whatever the storybook had said. It was the same with the footprints. The only vampire who ever had footprints which glowed was Sergio Snap and this was only for a short time. After he had been to a party one night and drunk a bit too much toadstool gin, he accidentally fell down the chimney of a nuclear power station. For several weeks afterwards, his entire body glowed and the astronomers became quite excited whenever Sergio flew anywhere. They thought they had discovered a new comet.

The Lasagnas had their stroke of luck while they were searching a wood near an old castle. Laszlo was fed up with looking down at the ground for luminous footprints, especially as this gave him a crick in the neck. He was having a rest when he noticed a bird flying overhead. 'Luigi,' he said. 'How big are seagulls.'

'I don't know,' his brother answered without looking up. 'I suppose it depends how much they eat.'

'Do they live in castles and have ugly scrvants who wave goodbye to them?'

'Of course they don't, stupid.'

'Oh.' Laszlo was disappointed. He didn't know the names of any other birds apart from seagulls. 'Well, what birds have glowing red eyes and dress themselves up in funny cloaks.'

'That isn't a bird, stupid. Only vampires have. . . .'

Suddenly Luigi wasn't looking down at the ground any more either. He was staring up at Blood Castle, jumping up and down with excitement as he watched Samuel Suck circling the battlements.

And two nights later, the same night that Igor tested the SALAD and Fenella gave Samuel his present, Spiro was on his way to join the Lasagnas. The special cage at the zoo was ready and he was coming to collect his vampire.

Three

No coffin was ever quite as comfortable as your own, Fenella thought to herself. Although Igor had smoothed down the earth in Uncle Samuel's spare coffin and dampened it nicely, it still wasn't the same as being at home in her own cosy crypt. In fact, Fenella hadn't slept at all well. She didn't usually dream a great deal but here at Uncle Samuel's she had had a strange daymare, something about humans creeping down into the dungeon and doing terrible things to her and her uncle while they were asleep. This probably had something to do with the weird noises which had helped to disturb her sleep. Fenella was used to the squeaking of the bats and rats in her own crypt, but here at Blood Castle everything was different. There had been bumps and crashes and the sound of somebody muttering; she supposed that Igor must have been tidying up.

Anyway, it would be getting dark outside by now. Although Fenella knew that Samuel would still be sleeping, there was nothing to stop her leaving her coffin. She could ask Igor to prepare her a snack while she was waiting for her uncle. Fenella pushed open the coffin lid and climbed out. Moving quietly, she started towards the steps leading from the dungeon; halfway up, she suddenly stopped. 'That's odd,' Fenella thought to herself. 'There's something different about the dungeon tonight.'

At first she thought Igor must have redecorated and she had been too tired to notice when she had gone to her coffin the previous morning. Looking around her, though, she could see that this wasn't the case: the same thumbscrews, chains and other decorations were still in their familiar places on the walls; nor had any of the cobwebs been rearranged. 'Something's different, though,' she muttered. 'Something isn't here that ought to be.'

Then Fenella realized what it was – her uncle's coffin seemed to have disappeared. The stone plinth on which it stood was still there, the outline of the coffin was clearly marked in the thick dust but there was no other sign of the coffin itself. Fenella couldn't understand this at all. Could it be Bladderwort Wally night already?

This night was when the younger vampires played silly tricks on everybody, like nailing down coffin lids or tying wings together. If their tricks worked, they would fly off laughing and shouting, 'Bladderwort Wally,' over their shoulders. But

Fenella knew Bladderwort was still several munches* away.

Her next thought was that Uncle Samuel might have been doing some experiments to make himself invisible. But when she went down to the plinth and felt around with her hands she discovered the coffin definitely wasn't there. Fenella was suddenly certain that something terrible must have happened to her uncle and she ran from the dungeon, calling for Igor at the top of her voice.

There was no answer at all. Apart from herself, Blood Castle seemed to be deserted. Running even faster now, Fenella rushed around the castle to check all the rooms and every one of them was empty. Both Samuel and his servant had completely vanished. By the time she returned to the Great Hall, Fenella was seriously concerned.

'Uncle! Igor! Where are you?' she called one last time. 'If you're hiding, you can come out now. It isn't funny.'

There was no reply; the castle was empty and silent around her. No, this wasn't quite true; vampires have very good hearing, far better than any human, and Fenella could faintly detect a scrabbling noise, the sort of sound which might be made by a large rat. It seemed to be coming from the kitchens and Fenella started running in this

*1 munch = 1½ human months

direction. As she drew closer, the mysterious sound not only became louder, it changed as well. Now there was a banging and a crashing; it sounded as though somebody had put their head inside a bucket and was knocking it against the wall.

'That's ridiculous,' Fenella said to herself as she raced along the corridor. 'Nobody could possibly be that stupid.'

By now she was close enough to realize the noises were coming from the broom cupboard just outside the kitchen. When she threw open the door she found Igor inside. He was rolling around on the floor with his head in a bucket which he was banging against the wall.

'What do you think you're doing, you silly little man,' she demanded sharply. 'Stop being so stupid at once.'

Igor didn't stop being stupid: he was making far too much noise to hear her. Apart from the bucket over his head, he had a large sack pulled over him which was tied at the waist and ankles. In fact, the only way Fenella could tell it really was Igor was by the smell and the shoes. They were the same shoes Igor had been wearing every day for the past twenty-nine years and, apart from being incredibly filthy, there were a lot of holes in them. Through these, Fenella could see patches of even filthier socks.

'This is no time for you to be in fancy dress, Igor,' Fenella told him.

As she spoke, Fenella bent down to give a sharp tug at the bucket. Unfortunately, Igor had been banging the bucket so hard that he had bent the metal and it was now stuck firmly on his head. Fenella gave another sharp tug but it still wouldn't shift. All that happened was that Igor started shouting something from inside. It sounded like, 'Aawwttiirrttss!'

'Either talk properly, Igor, or don't talk at all,' Fenella said. 'I'm not in the mood for your silly games.'

This time she held Igor's sack-covered body firmly between her knees so she could use both hands to pull at the bucket with all her strength.

'Aawwuurrppuulliinnmmiihheeddoorrff!' The bucket shifted slightly and then stuck again.

Next Fenella tried putting the bucket down on the floor so Igor was upside down. Gripping hold of the bucket with her feet, she took hold of Igor's legs. Vampires are very strong indeed and Fenella was pulling as hard as she possibly could.

'Aaaaaaaaawwwwwwww!'

'The idiot is singing to himself now,' Fenella muttered under her breath as she pulled. 'Falling into the moat must have given him water on the brain.'

With a sudden plop, Igor's head finally came free. It only took Fenella a few moments to undo the rope. When Igor's head emerged, it was so red it was almost purple. All the warts were glowing

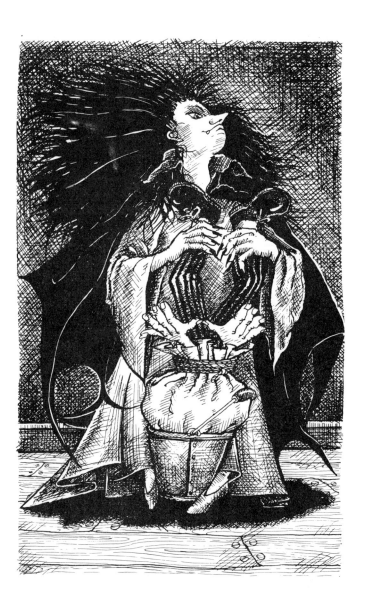

and there were tears in his eyes.

'Oh my poor head,' he moaned, clutching it with both hands. 'You nearly pulled my head off.'

'Don't be such a baby, Igor. Besides, it's your own silly fault for putting your head in a bucket in the first place.'

'I didn't, Mistress.'

Igor was making less fuss now he had discovered his nose and ear were still in place.

'How did it get there then? I suppose the bucket jumped up from the floor while you weren't looking.'

'Oh no, Mistress. It wasn't like that at all. I was attacked.'

'Attacked? What do you mean?'

Still very red in the face, Igor began to explain.

The knock at the front door of the castle had come early in the morning, shortly after Fenella and Samuel had retired to their coffins. Igor had shuffled off to answer it, muttering unpleasant words under his breath; he didn't welcome visitors at the best of times and he especially didn't welcome them just after he had nearly drowned testing the SALAD.

'Yes?' he snarled. 'What do you want?'

The man outside had taken a quick step backwards and put his hand up over his eyes. Nobody had warned him how hideous Igor was. 'I'm sorry to disturb you, sir,' he said, 'but I'm from the gas board. I've come to read your meter.'

'We don't have gas here. Clear off.' Igor had slammed the door in the man's face and was just shuffling off when there was another knock. Muttering even nastier words, Igor stormed back and threw the door open. 'I thought I told you . . .,' he had started angrily.

Then Igor had stopped because there was a different man standing on the doorstep. He looked even more stupid than the man from the gas board.

'Good morning. Ow my shins!'

To Igor's amazement, the man had bent over and started rubbing the fronts of his legs.

'My name's Igor,' he snapped, 'not ow my shins. What do you want?'

'I've come to read the electricity meter,' the man said in a rush.

'We don't have electricity here,' Igor had snarled.

He had been about to slam the door again when the man who had said he was from the gas board reappeared. He had been hiding behind the hedge. 'Wait a minute, sir,' he called as he ran forward. 'I have good news for you – very good news indeed. As you answered our two questions correctly, you win a prize.'

'What questions?' Igor was sure both men must be completely crazy.

'About the gas and electricity meters, sir. There's just one other little test and you win a magnificent prize.'

'What is it?' The man might be crazy but Igor liked the sound of a prize. He had never, ever won anything in his life.

'It's a . . . it's a . . . .'

'Has your needle stuck?'

'Oh no, sir. Before I tell you what our prize is, perhaps you'd like to tell me what you'd most like to win.'

'A Do-It-Yourself Torture Kit.' There was no hesitation at all: this was something Igor had wanted to win ever since he was a little boy.

'Now isn't that a coincidence, sir. That's exactly what our prize is.'

'What do I have to do?' Igor had said, dribbling with excitement. 'What's this test?'

'It's easy, sir. All you have to do is pull this sack on over your head in less than thirty seconds.'

At this point, Igor stopped his story. His face had gone very red again, this time the result of anger.

'Go on, Igor,' Fenella said. 'What happened next?'

'They cheated me, Mistress. I pulled the sack on

43

really fast but I didn't get a prize at all. One of them must have hit me because the next thing I remember is being tied up in here with a bucket on my head. They must have thought I was a real idiot.'

So did Fenella, although she didn't say so. She was far more concerned about her uncle. 'Do you have any idea what might have happened to Uncle Samuel?' she asked.

'The master?' Now Igor was sounding alarmed. 'Was he put into a sack too, Mistress?'

'I don't know, Igor. He's disappeared and so has his coffin. I think those men must have taken him away with them.'

'Why, Mistress?'

This was the question which was vexing Fenella. Why, in Drac's name, would anybody want to steal Uncle Samuel? Of course, Fenella had always known that humans were strange creatures with even stranger ideas about vampires. Humans were always trying to creep up on them while they were sleeping peacefully in their coffins. Then they would hammer stakes through their hearts or shoot them with silver bullets. Although nothing could kill a vampire the holes through the body were jolly inconvenient, especially in windy weather. Strange as they were, though, Fenella had never heard of humans stealing a vampire before. Perhaps they had just been

44

after the coffin and hadn't known Samuel was inside.

'What were these two men like?' Fenella asked.

'I didn't really notice, Mistress. They were both big and that's all I remember.'

Although this wasn't a great deal of help, Fenella wasn't really surprised. Apart from Igor and a little girl she had known once called Heinz Beans, all humans looked the same to her.

'There's one thing, Mistress. There was a lorry parked just down the road with another man sitting inside.'

'What's a lorry?'

'It's a big thing with a wheel at each corner. It's used for carrying goods around.'

'You mean good people?' There was a puzzled frown on Fenella's face. She was always having trouble with human words.

'No, Mistress. It carries things around which are too big for you to manage with your hands. It's rather like a great big hearse.'

'So the men could have put Uncle Samuel's coffin into it.'

'Yes, Mistress.'

Fenella was becoming excited. There were a lot of questions which remained to be answered but at least they had taken one small step in the right direction. 'Did you notice anything else, Igor?'

'Well, there was lots of writing on the side of the lorry.'

'What did it say?'

'It said . . . let me see.' Igor screwed up his face to help him concentrate – this made him look even more hideous than usual. 'That's right, Mistress. It said PA.'

'PA? What does that mean?'

'I don't know, Mistress.' Now Igor sounded miserable. 'There was a lot more writing as well but I didn't have time to read it all.' Igor was almost as bad at reading as he was at counting.

'Never mind, Igor. At least it gives us something to go on. I'm going to fly round and visit all my friends; I'll tell them what's happened and see if they have any suggestions.'

'What do you want me to do, Mistress?'

'You'd better stay here, Igor, just in case Uncle Samuel does return. I'll be back myself before morning.'

Although Fenella had tried to sound bright and cheerful while she was talking to Igor, it was a very worried vampire who flew away from Blood Castle. She was more certain than ever that something dreadful must have happened to Samuel and she had absolutely no idea what she could do.

Four

Samuel hadn't enjoyed a much better day's sleep than his niece, which was most unusual for him. For the past three hundred years or so, since he had started becoming really old, Samuel had been retiring to his coffin earlier and earlier in the morning and leaving it later and later at night. Sometimes he would even pop down to the dungeon for a quick snooze during the hours of darkness. As he had said to Fenella once, sleeping and inventing were about the only things he still did really well.

The previous day, however, Samuel had hardly done more than doze. Although he had never been completely awake, he didn't seem to have had any proper sleep at all. In fact, Samuel was sure he must be ill. If he hadn't known his coffin was standing safely in the dungeon of Blood Castle, he would have sworn he was suffering from coffin sickness, an illness vampires occasionally have when they are travelling long distances in a hearse.

As Samuel knew his coffin hadn't moved at all, it couldn't be this which was making him feel sick. At the same time, he couldn't think what other cause there could be. The only other real illness vampires suffered from was the purple palsy. Vampires who had this would feel really rotten, shaking all over while great purple blotches sprang up on their bodies. However, this was even less likely than coffin sickness, because only young vampires ever had the purple palsy. No vampire over a hundred and fifty had ever caught it. To be on the safe side, Samuel stuck out his tongue to check but it was a healthy greenish colour without a single purple blotch in sight. (Vampires have much longer tongues than humans so they never need a mirror to examine them.)

The only other possibility Samuel could think of was that he had some completely new disease. As he was by far the oldest vampire, it might be some illness you could only catch after you were over two thousand years old. 'That's the last thing I want to invent,' Samuel muttered to himself, 'coffin sickness without travelling anywhere.'

Lying around in his coffin wasn't likely to make his stomach feel any better so Samuel pushed open the lid. At first he wasn't aware of his surroundings. His mouth was opened in an enormous yawn, his eyes tightly closed, so it was the smell which first told him there was something wrong. There were a lot of strange scents in the air but one of them was unmistakeable. It was the smell of humans – not the nice, comfortable smell of Igor but the nasty, bitter odour other humans gave off.

When Samuel's eyes snapped open, there wasn't a human in sight. Even so the shock was enough to make him pinch himself to make sure he was awake. His coffin wasn't standing in the dungeon of Blood Castle any more. Instead, it was in the middle of a strange building Samuel had never seen before. There was a roof and three walls, one of them with a steel door in it, but where the fourth wall should have been, there were thick, iron bars. He was in a large cage and this was sufficient to make Samuel pinch himself again, just to make sure he hadn't dreamed that he'd pinched himself the first time.

'Ouch!' Samuel had pinched himself rather too hard. 'Well, I'm definitely not asleep. This really is most interesting – I wonder what's been happening.'

More curious than frightened, Samuel walked across to the door. Although there was a keyhole in it, there was no handle. That's a nuisance, he thought. I may have to knock the wall down when I want to leave. Let's have a look at those bars first, though.

He went to the front of the cage and took hold of two of them. When he pulled they started to bend. This was all Samuel needed to know – he could leave this way when he was ready to go. For the moment he simply wanted to have a good look around.

Peering out through the bars, Samuel could see several other cages, none of them quite as big as his. The only one he could see into was directly opposite, where a pair of large, yellowish eyes were staring back at him. The eyes belonged to a creature with a large yellowish body to match and a ruff of black hair around its neck. On the outside of the cage, there was a metal plaque saying, 'Lion'. Samuel assumed this must be short for Lionel.

'How do you do, Lionel,' he said politely. 'My name is Samuel and I'm very pleased to meet you.'

Lionel didn't seem to be at all pleased. He simply opened his mouth wide and roared fiercely.

'What terrible manners,' Samuel muttered, quite annoyed. 'Well, two can play that game.'

Although he couldn't open his mouth quite as wide, Samuel's roar was much, much louder. With a frightened yelp, Lionel jumped back from the bars and crouched shaking against the back wall of his cage. Samuel nodded in satisfaction and turned away – he wasn't going to waste any more time on the creature if he wasn't prepared to be friendly. Besides, all this roaring had made his coffin sickness twice as bad and it was high time he went home. Igor could come and collect the coffin later.

At more or less the same time that Samuel Suck had been waking up in his coffin, Spiro Pasta and the Lasagna brothers had been having a conference in the nearby mansion. He might have a vampire of his very own but Spiro still had a problem. 'The question is,' Spiro said. 'What do we feed him?'

'There's plenty of slippery spaghetti to spare, Boss,' Laszlo suggested.

'Don't be so stupid,' retorted Luigi. 'Vampires don't eat spaghetti. They need candied cherries and stewed prunes.'

'What did you say?' Spiro could hardly believe his ears.

'Candied cherries and stewed prunes, Boss,' Luigi said proudly. 'Vincent the Vampire was eating them all the time. Look, here's a picture of him having a snack.'

Luigi had quickly opened *Vincent the Vampire Goes to Mars* to the right page and was holding it out. After one glance at the picture, Spiro snatched the book from Luigi's hands and threw it into the fire. 'You fool,' he shouted. 'That's a kid's storybook. Real vampires aren't like that at all; they're big and fierce and they suck human blood.'

'Big and fierce, Boss?' Luigi's face had gone very white.

'Vampires are the fiercest creatures on earth,' Spiro told him. 'That's why I had to build a special cage.'

'A-a-and th-th-they s-suck b-b-blood?' Laszlo stammered, going even whiter.

'Human blood,' Spiro told him. 'That's why I'm worried about feeding him. How are we going to find enough human blood to keep him fit and healthy?'

Looking at the Lasagna brothers, Spiro knew where he could find at least two meals, but then he wouldn't have anybody to capture the other people he would need to feed the vampire. By now both Luigi and Laszlo were as white as sheets and trembling so much that their teeth were chattering. Although they were very good at bullying people smaller and weaker than themselves, they were also cowards. Neither of them would have gone anywhere near Blood Castle if they had realized how dangerous vampires could be.

'Come on you two,' Spiro said, rising to his feet. 'My vampire should be up and about now it's dark. Let's go and take a look at him.'

'I think I'll stay here, Boss.' Luigi was trembling more than ever. 'I've got a bad headache all of a sudden.'

'I must have caught mine from him,' Laszlo said. 'I'll stay here too.'

'Oh no you won't, you're both coming with me,' Spiro snarled. He was feeling nervous too and he certainly wasn't going to see the vampire on his own. 'There's no need to worry. The vampire can't get out of his cage and even if he could, I'll have this with me.'

Spiro patted the gun he had picked up from beside his chair. It shot a special tranquillizer dart which was guaranteed to put any animal to sleep in less than a second. When Spiro had tested it on an elephant, it had been fast asleep for eight days, snoring through its trunk. Just to be on the safe side, Spiro had doubled the dose for a vampire.

The three men had left the mansion and were walking through the zoo when the lion roared at Samuel. This was nothing unusual and it didn't bother them at all. What did bother them was the way Samuel roared back. It was a sound none of them had heard before – very few humans had – and it was enough to chill the blood in their veins.

'It's the vampire,' screamed Luigi.

'It's coming to get us,' screamed Laszlo.

Both of the Lasagna brothers started to run in terror and there was no saying how far they might have gone if they hadn't tried to run in opposite directions. As it was, they crashed straight into each other and fell to the ground in a struggling heap. This made a nice soft landing for Spiro who had jumped nine feet into the air when Samuel roared. If there had been anybody there to measure his leap, he would probably have got into the *Guinness Book of Records*.

Once they had fought their way back to their feet, the Lasagnas would have started running again if Spiro Pasta hadn't stopped them. Frightened as he was himself, he was determined to have his first look at the vampire. 'Get going, both of you,' he snarled, pointing the gun at them. 'Otherwise I'll make you the vampire's first meal.'

Reluctantly, the two brothers started walking towards Samuel's cage with Spiro several paces behind. If anything went wrong, Spiro intended to make sure he wasn't the one the vampire caught first.

Samuel Suck would already have left for Blood Castle if it hadn't been for his false teeth. He had been about to bend the bars apart so he could squeeze through when he had remembered them. 'I'd better not leave them behind,' he said to himself. 'It might be a night or two before Igor can collect my coffin; I'm bound to feel like a square meal before then.'

Samuel had just slipped the teeth into a pocket when he heard the sound of footsteps approaching. Three men were coming towards his cage, two large ones in front followed by a smaller, fatter one who was carrying a strangely shaped stick. Samuel shuddered at the sight of them. Their nasty, pink colour was so ugly compared with a vampire's beautiful greenish skin. He supposed Igor must be exceptionally good-looking for a human.

As he watched, it suddenly occurred to Samuel that these must be the humans who had dragged him from Blood Castle and shut him up in this ridiculous cage. They were the ones who were responsible for making him feel coffin sick. For the first time since he had woken up, Samuel began to feel angry. He didn't like humans at the best of times but this really was too much. By now the humans had stopped a few paces away from the cage and were staring at him.

'You miserable microbes,' Samuel hissed, red sparks flashing from his eyes.

All three men moved nervously backwards. The two in front looked as though they would have run away if the one at the back hadn't waved his stick at them.

'What's he talking about, Boss?' one of the big men asked shakily.

'I'm talking about you, idiot,' Samuel snapped. 'What's the meaning of it? That's what I want to know.'

None of the men attempted to reply. They simply stood where they were with their mouths hanging stupidly open.

'Won't answer, hey?' Samuel was becoming angrier by the moment. 'I think I'm going to teach you all a lesson before I fly home.'

'It's all right, boys,' the small, fat human said in a squeaky voice. 'He can't get out.'

'Oh can't he?' snarled Samuel. 'Just watch this.'

Spiro Pasta and the Lasagna brothers watched in horror as Samuel seized hold of the bars and started bending them as though they were made of Plasticine. They couldn't believe any creature could possibly be so strong. They would have liked to run from the furious old vampire before he was free but for the moment they were frozen to the spot by terror. The gap was almost large enough for Samuel to squeeze through before they started thinking again.

'The gun, Boss,' Luigi screeched. 'Use the gun.'

'Yes, yes, yes,' babbled Laszlo. 'Hit him with the gun.'

Samuel didn't pay much attention when the short, fat man lifted up his stick and pointed it at him. Although he had heard about guns, he had never seen one before so it was quite a surprise when there was a loud bang and something pricked him in the chest. When he looked down there was a kind of large needle sticking out of him. Samuel simply pulled it free, threw it on to the floor and turned back to the bars. It would take more than a

56

big needle to make him change his mind. He still intended to get out of this cage and teach those horrible, little humans a much-needed lesson. Or did he? Suddenly Samuel was feeling tired – very, very tired indeed. His mouth opened in a huge yawn. It really would be such an effort to bend the bars and punish those silly humans. He could easily do it later after he had had a little snooze and wasn't feeling quite so weary. With a last, fierce glare at the three men, Samuel turned away and walked slowly to his coffin.

'I'll deal with you later,' he mumbled as the coffin lid closed with a crash behind him.

After the vampire had vanished into his coffin, nobody spoke for a few moments. Spiro was still trembling so much that the rings on his fingers clanged together and both the Lasagnas were as white as sheets again. They all knew they had been very, very lucky.

'I thought he couldn't get out of the cage, Boss,' Luigi said in a shaky voice. His knees had been knocking so hard that he had bruises on them.

'So did I,' Spiro told him. 'We'll have to make it even stronger.'

'What if he wakes up before the cage is ready?' Laszlo asked. 'I could be wrong but I don't think that vampire liked us very much.'

'If he wakes up too soon, we'll put him to sleep again the moment he opens his coffin.' Spiro was more excited than frightened by now. He was already thinking about his favourite subject, money. 'We're going to make a fortune out of him, even more than we've made from slippery spaghetti. There's nothing people like more than something really scarey. If they'll pay to see mangy old lions and tigers and polar bears just think what they'll hand over to see a hideous vampire with glowing red eyes and great white teeth that could rip them into shreds. Why, they'll—'

Spiro suddenly stopped, knowing there was something wrong with what he had just said about the vampire. Slowly he went over it again in his head. The vampire was certainly hideous all right. In fact, it was so ugly it almost made the Lasagnas seem good-looking. And he hadn't been wrong about the eyes either. Spiro had felt as though they were burning into him when the vampire had looked in his direction. And everybody knew about a vampire's teeth. Even Vincent had had them in that stupid book Luigi had stolen from the library. Then Spiro remembered the vampire yawning. His mouth had opened so wide it had looked like a tunnel and tunnels didn't have teeth.

'You idiots,' he screamed at Luigi and Laszlo. 'You incompetent imbeciles.'

The brothers watched in amazement as Spiro threw his gun on the floor and did a kind of war dance on it. As Spiro danced, he moaned and as he moaned, he tore great handfuls of hair from his head.

'You're making yourself bald, Boss,' Luigi said anxiously.

'Perhaps there's something the matter,' Laszlo suggested.

'Of course there's something the matter, you great twerp,' Spiro yelled, frothing at the mouth. 'Go and open the coffin.'

'But . . . .'

'Open the coffin I said.'

Spiro had picked up his gun again and was pointing it straight at Laszlo. For the moment he looked as dangerous as any vampire and Laszlo did as he was told. To his relief, Samuel was fast asleep, snoring peacefully.

'Now open the mouth,' Spiro ordered.

Laszlo opened his mouth as wide as he could.

'Not your mouth, idiot,' Spiro screamed. 'Open the vampire's mouth.'

Taking hold of Samuel's nose and chin, Laszlo nervously pulled his mouth open. Then he looked across at Spiro for further instructions.

'What can you see?' Spiro asked.

'A vampire in a coffin with his mouth open.' Laszlo was pleased at this easy question.

'That's not what I meant. What's inside the vampire's mouth?'

'Well, there's a tongue – it's all green and pointed.

59

Then there's gums and a big, black hole and—'

'How many teeth are there?' Spiro interrupted with a snarl.

'There aren't any teeth.'

'Exactly.' Spiro was screaming again and his face had turned purple with rage. 'You two fools have captured a vampire without any teeth. What use is that to me? How can he bite into anybody's neck without any teeth? I can just see the notice on his cage. "Keep well back. This vampire can give you a nasty suck." That should really scare people.'

'I don't understand it, Boss.' Luigi had joined his brother inside the cage to check for himself. Even when he tugged Samuel's cheeks back he failed to find a single tooth. 'The other vampire at the castle had lots of teeth.'

'That's right,' Laszlo agreed. 'Great, sparkling white choppers they were. I remember thinking how much toothpaste she must use.'

'Why didn't you bring her instead of that useless thing in the coffin. A toothless vampire is about as much use as an elephant without a trunk or a tortoise without a shell,' roared Spiro.

'I'm sorry, Boss.'

'Sorry isn't good enough. You can jolly well go back to the castle and catch me a proper vampire.'

Both of the brothers started shaking their heads together: now they knew how dangerous vampires could be, they had no intention of going near Blood Castle again. It didn't matter how much Spiro threatened or shouted at them, they wouldn't change their minds. Spiro was still arguing with them when an idea suddenly occurred to him: it was such a good idea that his face split into a broad smile. (It wasn't a pretty smile, nothing about Spiro's face was very pretty.)

'I've got it,' he shouted delightedly, making the brothers jump.

61

'What, Boss?' Luigi asked.

'I know how to capture the other vampire: we'll make it come here to us.'

'How will we manage that, Boss?'

Still smiling, Spiro began to explain his plan.

Five

None of the friends Fenella visited had seen Uncle Samuel, nor did they have any idea what could have happened to him. They all said they had never heard of humans stealing a vampire before and it made no more sense to them than it had to Fenella.

As the night wore on, her only hope was that Samuel might have returned to Blood Castle while she was away. When she got back just before morning though, one look at Igor's face was sufficient to tell her the worst: Igor had seen no sign of his master either.

For a long time Fenella tossed and turned in her coffin while she thought about the strange series of events. No matter how much she thought, she came no closer to an explanation for them. Worse still, she had no real idea how to set about finding her uncle. The only clues she had were the two men who had tied Igor in a sack and the lorry with PA written on the side. This wasn't a great deal to go on and she wished she knew more about humans.

It was the middle of the day before Fenella finally fell into an exhausted sleep, only to have the worst daymare she could remember. It was filled with ugly humans who had crept back to Blood Castle to steal her as well. The worst moment was when the humans came into the dungeon and began nailing down the lid of her coffin. This part of the daymare was so real that Fenella woke with a start, the banging still ringing in her ears. It continued even after she was awake when, to her horror, Fenella realized the banging was no dream. Somebody really was nailing her into her coffin.

The horror suddenly gave way to anger. 'The nerve of it,' she muttered furiously. 'I'll show those interfering humans what happens when they mess with vampires.'

With one enormous heave, Fenella threw open the lid of the coffin, pushing so hard that the lid almost came off its hinges. Still half asleep, she saw the man standing beside the coffin, his hand raised. With an angry roar, Fenella lashed out with one arm, hitting him so hard that he shot backwards across the dungeon until he crashed into the wall at the far end. It was only then that she saw who she had hit. 'Oh Igor,' she cried, starting to scramble out of the coffin. 'I didn't know it was you. Are you all right?'

'I'm fine, Mistress,' Igor answered shakily, climbing unsteadily back to his feet. 'I only banged my head a little.'

In a few seconds, Igor had completely recovered from the shock. Although there was a nasty bump on his head where it had hit the wall, it hardly showed amongst the warts which were already there.

'Why were you banging on the coffin?' she asked, once she was sure Igor had recovered.

'It's good news, Miss Fenella.' Igor was suddenly all smiles. 'While you've been asleep I've found the master.'

'That's wonderful, you clever old thing.' Fenella was so delighted by the news that she lifted Igor into the air and nuzzled his neck. 'Where is Uncle Samuel? Is he upstairs in the Great Hall?'

'No, Mistress. When I said I'd found him, I didn't mean he was actually here. I meant I know where he is.'

'Well, that's almost as good and I'm really proud of you.' Fenella nuzzled Igor again. 'Where did those horrible men take him?'

'To a zoo.'

'Azoo? Isn't that what you do when you sneeze?'

'No, Mistress. A zoo is a place where lots of different animals are kept in cages and people pay to go and look at them.'

'You mean they took Uncle Samuel to look at the animals?'

Igor shook his head so hard that it was surrounded by a great cloud of dandruff. 'They've put the master in a cage too.'

'But he isn't an animal – he's a vampire.' Fenella was absolutely horrified. 'Why would they want to do that?'

'I don't know, Miss Fenella.'

'Well, we can sort that out when we bring him back here. First of all, I want to hear how you discovered where those humans took him.'

'There wasn't anything to it, Mistress. It was easy.'

'That's what you say but I'm sure you're just being modest. Tell me how you did it.' Fenella was feeling quite proud of Igor. He was obviously much cleverer than she had ever given him credit for.

'It was after you went to your coffin this morning, Miss Fenella. I sat down to think of all the places the Master might have been taken to.'

'And that was when you had your idea about the zoo.'

'No, not quite. I didn't have any ideas at all.'

Igor had stopped again and Fenella was becoming confused. 'What happened then?' she asked.

'I fell fast asleep,' Igor said. 'I must have slept most of the day.'

'I know, I know.' Fenella could see what had happened now. 'You had a dream about a zoo.'

'No, I never dream, Mistress.'

'So how did you find out, Igor?' By now Fenella was becoming quite exasperated.

'Like I said, Miss Fenella, it was easy: somebody pushed this under the door while I was asleep.'

Igor pulled a folded and creased piece of paper from his pocket, along with a lot of fluff and some stale chewing gum. Once Fenella had smoothed it out and unstuck the gum, she could see it was a poster. 'Pasta's zoo', it said. 'The finest in the land. Come and see the only vampire in captivity – so hideous he'll make your blood run cold.' Underneath this was a photograph of Samuel asleep in his coffin and a little map showing how to reach the zoo. Although she was most relieved to know her uncle was safe, Fenella was becoming more and more angry. How dare these humans steal Samuel and put him on display with a lot of animals? How dare they say he was hideous?

'Shall we go and bring the master back now?' Igor asked. He was beginning to dribble the way he always did when he was excited.

'What do *you* think?' Fenella was already striding angrily towards the battlements and rescuing Samuel wasn't the only thought on her mind. She was in just the mood to teach those interfering humans a lesson they would never forget.

'There it is, Miss Fenella.'

It was a clear, moonlight night and from his perch on Fenella's back Igor could see the zoo spread out far below them. Fenella made no attempt to land immediately. Instead, she flew

above the cages and enclosures in a great circle, staring downwards as though she was trying to see where Samuel was being held captive. Then she flew around again before she spoke. 'Hold on tight, Igor,' she said. 'I'm going down now.'

Igor didn't like landings and he closed his eyes, not opening them again until they were safely on the ground. To his surprise, the zoo was nowhere in sight. They were in the middle of a large empty field. 'You missed, Mistress.'

Igor thought Fenella must have had her eyes closed too.

'Of course I didn't. This was where I meant to land.'

Although Igor would have liked to ask her why, there was no chance. As soon as he had climbed from her back, Fenella began walking up the hill in front of them. Igor lurched after her, keeping up as best he could. His different-sized legs made walking uphill difficult at the best of times. Tonight it was especially awkward because of the tools he had brought with him to help with the escape; shovels and grapnels and dynamite and useful things like that. When he eventually

reached the top of the hill, he was quite out of breath.

'What are you doing, Mistress?' he asked once he could speak.

'I'm thinking, Igor.'

For a while Igor stood beside her, looking down at the zoo, and tried to do the same. The trouble was, all he could think of was ice cream which was one of his favourite foods. He couldn't see how this would help the master.

'That poster was a trick,' Fenella said at last.

'How could it be, Mistress?' Igor didn't understand what she was talking about. 'It was the master's photograph all right. I'd recognize him anywhere.'

'So would I, Igor. The question I keep asking myself is why did they send the poster to Blood Castle. They know that was where Uncle Samuel was stolen from.'

'They would have printed thousands of posters, Mistress. They probably sent one to every house in the country.'

'How do you explain the map then?'

Igor couldn't, not even when Fenella pulled the poster out of her pocket and showed it to him. He didn't understand maps at all and, in any case, the writing was far too small for him to read. It wasn't until Fenella pointed out that the only places shown on the map were Blood Castle and the zoo that he realized why she was suspicious. 'That is strange, Miss Fenella,' he agreed.

'There's more, Igor. Just look at these directions. It says here, "Fly straight ahead and watch out for your wings on the church steeple." And where it shows the zoo it says, "You can land right in front of the vampire's cage." Do humans fly when they go to the zoo?'

A great cloud of dandruff drifted down to the grass as Igor shook his head. 'Not that I know of, Mistress.'

'Exactly. It's a trap. Those horrible humans expected me to rush straight to the zoo without thinking what I was doing.'

'Perhaps they want to capture you as well, Miss Fenella.'

'I think you're right. They're probably waiting for us in the zoo at this very moment. We need to make a plan.'

It was then, standing there on the hill above the zoo, that Igor had his idea. This only happened once every few years and most of his ideas were pretty stupid; however, this one was absolutely brilliant. 'They'll be expecting you to go to the zoo at night, Mistress,' he said excitedly. 'All humans know that's when vampires come out of their coffins. They don't know about the master's cream and goggles – you'll be able to go to the zoo during the day and take them completely by surprise.'

'You're right, Igor. Why didn't I think of that?'

Now Fenella was excited too. One of Uncle

Samuel's inventions had been a special cream which enabled vampires to go out on even the sunniest days provided they wore goggles to protect their eyes. Fenella had used the cream herself when she had visited a human dentist and it had worked perfectly. However, there were still problems.

'I'll have to wear a disguise,' she said. 'I don't want people to know I'm a vampire.'

'You've done it before, Miss Fenella. You can do it again.'

'I'll need somebody to go with me as well. Otherwise I won't know how to behave at the zoo. Humans have such strange customs.'

'I'll come with you, Mistress.'

'You can't, Igor. You know I'd rather have you with me than anybody but those men who stole Uncle Samuel have seen you; they'll recognize you at once.'

'I can wear a disguise too.'

'No, it's too much of a risk.'

For a few moments they were both silent. It seemed as though their plan wouldn't work after all. Fenella knew she could never manage at the zoo on her own, but the only other human she knew apart from Igor was only a child. If those men would steal a vampire, there was no saying what they might do to Heinz Beans (that was her name).

Fenella was thinking they might have to change their plan yet again when the solution to the problem suddenly occurred to her. 'I know where I can find a human,' she cried, her face brightening. 'I'm sure he'll be only too glad to help. You wait here, Igor, and keep an eye on the zoo. I'll be back before morning.'

Without another word to the bewildered servant, Fenella soared up into the sky. She did hope the human she was thinking of hadn't gone away.

'Rock-a-bye Bungle in the tree top,' Bert sang to himself. 'When the wind blows, the Bungle will rock.'

He thought this was so funny that he had to stop singing while he laughed and it was several seconds before he could stop giggling. Going without anything to eat or drink for such a long time had made him quite light-headed. 'You are a card, Bert Bungle,' he said, still chuckling. 'You should be on "Top of the Pops", not on top of an oak tree.'

For a few minutes he simply hung there by his belt, swaying gently in the breeze. It was dark again and Bert was trying to work out whether this was the second or third night he had spent in the tree. Hard as he tried, he simply couldn't remember. All he knew was that it had been an awfully long time and he was cold, hungry and thirsty. Bert felt so sorry for himself he could feel the tears beginning to prickle in his eyes.

'Look on the bright side, Bert,' he muttered

fiercely. 'Think of all the things you've learned about nature. Why, you're an expert now – you could go and give lectures.'

Birds were what he had learned about mostly. Bert had been able to observe a great spotted woodpecker really closely while it spent most of one day trying to drill holes in his left leg. Then there were the sparrows which had been using his hair to make their nests more comfortable. If he had had a mirror, he would have been able to check whether he was completely bald yet. Bert was sure he must be. The last sparrow to come visiting hadn't pulled out any hair at all, it had done something unpleasant on his head instead.

There had been plenty of other woodland creatures to study as well. By crossing his eyes, he had had a very clear view of the wasp which had stung him on the nose. And Bert had never realized before that squirrels would try to store their acorns in somebody's ears. Although he had shaken his head as hard as he dared, he was sure there were one or two acorns still stuck in there.

Thinking about nature wasn't doing anything to make Bert more cheerful, so he tried singing again. 'Rock-a-bye Bungle in the tree top, when the wind blows the Bungle will rock,' he warbled. 'When the belt breaks Bungle will fall, down will come Bungle, trousers and all.'

This time Bert didn't find the song at all amusing. Tears were beginning to well up in his eyes again when he heard the sounds of a large creature flying towards him. It came as no real surprise to see the vampire hovering in front of him, eyes shining in the darkness. The only surprising thing was that Bert didn't feel at all frightened; there was nothing the vampire could possibly do to him that was worse than what had already happened.

'Hello, Vampire,' he said. 'It's nice of you to come visiting. I was beginning to feel a bit lonely.'

'I wasn't sure whether you'd still be here.'

'Oh, yes,' Bert told her. 'I've just been hanging around.' He was feeling light-headed again and he thought his joke was so funny he would have laughed himself right out of the tree if Fenella hadn't been there to catch him.

'Are you all right?' she asked anxiously.

'Oh yes,' Bert said. 'There's nothing I enjoy more than being stuck in a tree for days on end without anything to eat or drink.'

'So you don't want me to take you down?' Fenella didn't understand human jokes and she had never heard of sarcasm. 'You're quite happy to stay where you are?'

'Of course I'm not happy,' Bert screamed in a panic, afraid that Fenella would fly away again. 'I hate it up here. It's horrible.'

'Why didn't you say so in the first place?'

'I'm sorry, I'm sorry,' Bert babbled. 'Please take me down from here. I'll do anything you want, anything at all.'

'Will you take me to the zoo?'

'I will, I will. I'll even pay for you to get in.' At that moment Bert would have promised anything. It was only later, as Fenella flew away with him clinging nervously to her back, that Bert began to wonder what on earth she had been talking about.

Six

Fenella was sure she would never, ever understand humans. Any vampire would simply have flown straight into the zoo but humans preferred to stand in a long line, shuffling forward a step at a time just so they could play some silly game at a little booth called, 'Ticket Office'. Nobody even looked happy while they were pushing metal discs and pieces of paper backwards and forwards. As if this didn't waste enough time, there was a revolving gate as well which was called a ternwhile or something equally stupid. Fenella would simply have jumped over it but Bert stopped her. She went round eight times before she finally managed to escape.

To begin with, Fenella hated it inside the zoo. There were hundreds of humans scuttling noisily around and they were such ugly creatures, Fenella soon felt quite ill. Gradually, however, she became used to them. For all their strange ways and horrible appearance their manners were very good. The humans must have realized how uncomfortable their hubbub was making her because they all fell silent when they saw Fenella coming. Most of them even moved out of her way so she had plenty of room. Fenella thought this was most considerate, although she couldn't think why so many of the younger humans started crying.

Nearly all the animals in the cages and enclosures were completely new to Fenella. As vampires usually only travel at night, they never see the creatures which are out and about during the daytime. Come to that, they don't often see nocturnal animals either because most of them are even more frightened of vampires than humans.

Fenella would have liked to examine some of the creatures more closely while she had the opportunity but she found this rather difficult. As soon as she went near the bars, the animals ran away to burrow in the straw at the back of their cages or hide in their sleeping quarters. Only the chimpanzees were friendly; they were so pleased to see her, they jumped up and down and screeched and threw pieces of rotten fruit at her.

After a time, Fenella became so interested in all the new sights around her that she began to forget why she had come to the zoo. It was Bert who reminded her. 'I don't see any vampires,' he said. 'Are you sure we've come to the right zoo?'

'Of course we have. Let's take a look at the map.' Fenella pulled the poster from her pocket and examined it. 'That's right. We'll find Uncle Samuel by the lion, whatever that is.'

'It's up this way,' Bert told her, pointing to a signpost.

They followed the path and it wasn't very long before they were standing outside the lion's cage. Fenella wasn't at all impressed by the creature: it looked like a cowardly animal, lying at the back of its cage and whining pitifully. According to the map, Samuel Suck was directly opposite but a tarpaulin had been fixed over the front of the cage where he should have been and it was impossible to see inside.

'All the cages have doors at the back,' Bert said. 'Let's go and take a look.'

Although there was a door, it was firmly locked. However, this was no problem to an ex-burglar like Bert. 'I could open this with my eyes closed,' he boasted. 'Just leave it to me. You go round the front and let me know if anyone is coming and I'll give you a shout as soon as the door is unlocked.'

After Fenella had gone, Bert looked around for a few moments. Now he was on his own, he had his big chance to escape. Bert had had a miserable time traipsing around the zoo. He knew all the other visitors had been pointing at him and the vampire and laughing at him behind his back. Some of them had even thought Fenella must be his wife. What with the oak tree and Blood Castle and this visit to the zoo, Bert had had more than enough. There was nothing he would have liked better than to clear off while he had the opportunity but he wasn't quite brave enough. For a start, he knew Igor was waiting outside the zoo. And even if he did manage to avoid Igor, Bert didn't want an angry vampire knocking at his door one dark night. It was far better to do as he had promised. Reluctantly, Bert started to work on the lock.

There was one important fact Spiro Pasta hadn't known when he had shot Samuel Suck with the tranquillizer drug: vampires never use any kinds of medicine and because their bodies are so different, drugs don't have the same effect on them as they do on people. Giving a vampire a drug is like making a human drink a bottle of whisky. The tranquillizer dart would have sent a man to sleep for several weeks but Samuel had only slept for just over twenty-four hours. He was already wide awake and he was feeling absolutely marvellous, chortling happily to himself as he planned what he intended to do. Inside his coffin, old Samuel was as drunk as a skunk and loving every moment of it. The only thought on his mind was mischief.

Careful not to make a sound, Samuel pushed up the coffin lid and peered out. Through the crack, he could see that Luigi Lasagna was fast asleep in his chair, snoring loudly with the tranquillizer gun resting against his leg. Although Luigi was supposed to be on guard, he didn't expect the vampire to wake up for at least another week and he was catching up on a bit of shuteye. Samuel had to close the lid again while he had a quick giggle– Luigi was about to have the shock of his life.

Samuel opened the coffin lid again. Although it creaked slightly, this did nothing to disturb Luigi's slumbers. Walking on tiptoe, Samuel moved silently across the darkened cage until he could reach the gun. Still moving without a sound, apart from the occasional hiccup of laughter, Samuel tiptoed back to the coffin and dropped the gun inside. There was only one thing left to do. Bending down at the sleeping man's feet, he quickly tied Luigi's shoelaces together. By now Samuel was laughing so much inside that he had a pain in his stomach. He had to lean against the bars of the cage for a while to recover.

'Dear, oh dear,' he chortled. 'I do wish Fenella was here to see this.'

The best was still to come. Standing behind the snoring Luigi, Samuel put his mouth close to his ear. 'Wakey, wakey,' he cooed.

Luigi woke up with a start, not sure what had disturbed him. It didn't take him long to find out. Even in the darkened cage, he could see that the lid of the coffin was open– a sight which made his blood run cold. Not taking his eyes off the coffin, Luigi reached out for the gun beside him, but it wasn't there! He was just wondering what to do when everything went black as a cold, scaly hand covered his eyes.

'Guess who's got a vampire right behind him,' Samuel warbled.

'Oh no,' Luigi screamed.

'Oh yes,' Samuel screamed back.

The terrified Luigi leapt from the chair and started to run for the door, but with his laces tied together, he didn't get very far. In fact, he only managed one step before he tripped and fell, banging his nose painfully on the floor. Behind him, Samuel was laughing so much at the success of his trick that he had fallen over as well.

'Help,' Luigi shouted, starting to crawl across the floor. 'Help me somebody. I'm being attacked by a hideous vampire.'

At least, Luigi had intended to shout but the best he could manage was a squeak.

'Help,' roared Samuel, showing Luigi how it should be done. 'Help him somebody. I'm attacking a horrible human.'

'Save me,' squeaked Luigi.

'Save him,' roared Samuel, getting to his feet and going to stand over Luigi.

Looking up at the terrible, menacing figure above him, Luigi lost his voice altogether. Although his lips continued to move, no sounds were coming out. Laughing happily, Samuel bent down and picked up the struggling man in one hand. 'Speak up,' he said. 'Surely you can do better than that.'

But Luigi couldn't. He had fainted and even when Samuel shook him, he didn't wake up.

'Rotten spoilsport,' Samuel said disappointedly. 'Just when we were having fun.' He dropped Luigi into the coffin, closed it and sat on the lid while he decided what to do next. Samuel was still feeling wonderful and now there wasn't anybody for him to play with. It just wasn't fair.

'Lionel,' he said suddenly, leaping to his feet. 'I can go and see Lionel. I bet he'll be pleased to see me.' But Samuel had only taken a couple of steps towards the bars when a noise stopped him in his tracks. Unless he was very much mistaken, somebody was undoing the lock on the door.

Bert Bungle had heard the disturbance on the other side of the door and his first thought had been to run. In fact, he had already taken several paces before he wondered exactly where he was going to run to – there wasn't much point in running from one vampire to another, especially when the other had a revolting human helper lurking somewhere nearby. Besides, the noises had only lasted for a few seconds. Now everything was quiet again.

'You've only got to fiddle the lock, Bert,' he

said, to give himself courage. 'Nobody said anything about going inside the cage. Once that door is open, you're finished. You'll never, ever have to see another vampire.'

Fortunately, the lock was a simple one and it was only a few seconds before it clicked free. Keeping a firm grip on the handle so the door wouldn't swing open, he turned to call for Fenella. At the same moment, Samuel Suck, still filled with mischief and merriment, hooked a finger into the keyhole from the inside. The first Bert knew of this was when the door was suddenly pulled open and as he was still holding on to the handle, Bert went with the door.

Before he knew it, Bert was in the last place he wanted to be; inside the cage staring up at the tall, gaunt figure of Samuel Suck. The old vampire's welcoming smile was supposed to be a friendly one. To Bert, it was absolutely terrifying and, for a moment, he was frozen to the spot. Only for a moment, though, because Samuel felt like some exercise after his long rest.

Before Bert had a chance to speak, Samuel had seized hold of him and was swinging him around the cage in a Transylvanian Toothdance. Like most vampire dances this was very energetic, involving a lot of prancing and leaping, and Bert was so shaken up he didn't even have the breath to scream.

There was no saying how long Bert's ordeal

might have lasted – sometimes a Toothdance could continue all night – if Fenella hadn't appeared in the doorway. She had come to see how Bert was doing with the lock and for a moment she couldn't believe the scene which greeted her. She was sure Samuel must have gone completely mad. 'What are you doing, Uncle?' she asked in bewilderment as Samuel swung round to face her.

'I'm tripping the light fantastic, dear.' Samuel's smile grew even broader as he recognized his favourite niece. 'Why don't you come and join in. We're having a lovely time.' Samuel was still rather the worse for wear and the effects of the tranquillizer were showing no signs of wearing off. He tossed the terrified Bert so high in the air that his head banged on the ceiling before Samuel caught him again on the way down.

'Stop it,' Fenella told him. 'Let go of poor Bert at once.'

It was Bert's bad luck that Samuel had been swinging his partner around his head when Fenella spoke. And as soon as Samuel let go of him, Bert flew all the way across the cage, hitting the bars so hard that his head jammed between two of them. Meanwhile, Samuel continued to dance on his own, twirling and jumping as though he were four or five centuries younger.

'Uncle Samuel,' Fenella said desperately, wondering what could have come over him, 'please be

careful or you'll hurt yourself. Besides, we have to be going. I've come to take you back to Blood Castle.'

'Blood Castle?' Samuel repeated, stopping in mid twirl. 'Blood Castle? That sounds familiar.'

'It's where you live, Uncle.'

'That accounts for it then, my bumptious little bat. I knew I'd heard the name somewhere. I'll just say goodbye to Lionel and we'll be off.' He started scuttling towards the door so fast that Fenella only just managed to grab his arm before he left the cage.

'It's the middle of the day, Uncle,' she told him. 'You can't go outside in your dayshroud.'

'Silly old me,' Samuel cackled, slapping himself playfully on the wrist. 'Whatever am I thinking of? I'll slip your dress on – the colour should suit me.'

'No, Uncle,' Fenella said, pushing him away. 'There are plenty of clothes in the drawers of your coffin, and you'll need some day-cream and goggles as well.'

'Anything you say, my toothsome one.'

Once she was sure that Samuel was dressing himself properly, Fenella turned her attention to Bert. He was moaning to himself as he lay on the floor with his head stuck firmly between the bars. 'Are you all right?' Fenella asked anxiously.

'Oh yes,' he told her. 'I always moan when I'm really happy.'

'You don't look very comfortable,' Fenella said doubtfully.

'Of course I'm not comfortable,' Bert screamed, tears springing into his eyes. 'I'm in agony. I'll probably have to spend the rest of my life with my head sticking out of a vampire's cage.'

'Don't be so silly. I'll have you free in a couple of snaps.'

It wasn't as easy as Fenella had expected. Spiro Pasta had had the bars strengthened again and it was all Fenella could do to move them at all. However, she refused to give in and Bert's head had just popped free when she heard the screams from outside. At the same moment, she realized Uncle Samuel was being suspiciously quiet. A quick glance over her shoulder confirmed her worst fears – Samuel was no longer in the cage. The only sign he had ever been there was the crumpled dayshroud on the floor.

There were more screams from outside as Fenella scrambled to her feet. She rushed from the cage in such a hurry that she didn't even have time to thank Bert. Not that Bert minded: he was only too glad to see the back of Fenella and her crazy uncle.

'Good riddance to them both, I say,' he muttered, giving his injured head a last rub. 'If I never see either of them again, that'll be far too soon.'

It was high time he was off too, Bert decided.

He had done his bit to help. Besides, it was rather spooky in the darkness of the cage, sitting there with a coffin for company. In the dim light he kept imagining the lid of the coffin was moving. Then Bert realized that he wasn't imagining anything – the coffin lid had lifted and a pair of eyes were peeping out at him.

'Is it safe to come out yet?' something in the coffin asked in a hoarse whisper.

With a blood-curdling scream which was far louder than any of those from outside, Bert leapt to his feet and ran from the cage without a backward glance. A few seconds later, Luigi Lasagna had scrambled out of the coffin and was running from the cage himself. He had to tell Spiro Pasta that his vampire had escaped.

'It's not fair,' Igor complained. 'Why should they have all the fun?'

As he was talking to himself, there was nobody to give him an answer. Igor had been waiting outside the zoo for hours and he was feeling miserable. Not that he was very happy at the best of times. The only things which really cheered him up were pulling the wings off flies or seeing somebody have a nasty accident, like slipping over on a banana skin.

As if hanging around the zoo entrance wasn't bad enough, some boys had upset Igor too. They had been playing football nearby and one of them had shouted out to ask Igor if it wasn't time he went back to his cage. All the horrible little brats had found this absolutely hilarious. Later on, though, Igor had had his revenge – when their football had come bouncing towards him, he had kicked it into the middle of the road where it was squashed flat by a lorry. This had made Igor feel a lot better, especially as the boys had run off crying.

By now, though, Igor was fed up again. He wanted to help to rescue his master.

'I could disguise myself as well as anyone,' he muttered darkly. 'I could dress up as Superman or something.'

Just then there was a commotion at the gate leading into the zoo and a man came rushing out, running as though his life depended on it. Igor recognized Bert Bungle at once. Although he shouted out to him, Bert didn't even turn his head and he was running far too fast for Igor to have any hope of catching him.

'Something must have gone wrong,' Igor said, beginning to dribble with excitement. 'I've got to do something to help.'

Seven

Ever since he had been a boy, Igor had wanted to drive a bus. Whenever he travelled on one, he always sat as close to the driver as possible so he could watch what had to be done. In this way, Igor had learned a lot. He knew there was one pedal to make the bus go faster, another to make it stop and a horn you blew when you wanted to make old ladies fall off their bikes. There were also a couple of sticks beside the driver's seat which Igor wasn't so sure about. Although he had seen the drivers play with them from time to time, he had no idea what they did. All the same, Igor was certain they couldn't be very important and he just knew he could drive a bus as well as anyone.

In fact, there was only one thing which puzzled him. On all the buses he saw going by, the drivers always held the wheel with both hands. Yet when he was sitting near them, the drivers used one hand to hold their noses. Igor couldn't be sure whether this helped them to drive or not but he decided to hold his nose anyway, just to be on the safe side.

There were several empty coaches in the car park. Igor chose one which had been left unlocked and scrambled up into the driving seat. Holding his nose with one hand and the steering wheel with the other, Igor stamped down hard on the go fast pedal. To his amazement, absolutely nothing happened. 'That's strange,' he muttered.

Then the answer occurred to him. 'It's the cap,' he said. 'All bus drivers wear one.'

Fortunately, the driver had left his cap hanging on a peg beside the seat. Although it was a bit on the large side and stopped him from seeing very well, Igor put it on, only to discover it didn't make any difference: the coach still wasn't moving.

For a while Igor tried jumping up and down on all the pedals and waggling the sticks but all to no avail. The only thing which worked was the horn and this wasn't much good because there wasn't an old lady on a bicycle anywhere in sight. Igor was about to give up when he noticed the small key in the dashboard in front of him. After he turned it, the engine spluttered into life and the whole coach shuddered before everything went quiet again.

Igor turned the key once more, this time with his foot on the go fast pedal. The engine worked all right but, to Igor's astonishment, all the other vehicles in the car park seemed to shoot forward while his own coach stayed where it was. 'That's very, very strange,' he said.

It took a few moments before Igor realized he had been mistaken. None of the other cars and buses were really moving at all – his own coach was shooting backwards. Before he could do anything about this, there was a loud crash as he hit the back of the coach parked behind him and came to a sudden halt.

'That's the bus I should have used,' Igor decided, looking back over his shoulder.

The other coach had been parked at the top of a slope and, as Igor watched, it trundled gently downhill. He waggled the sticks some more before he tried the key yet again and this time everything worked. Now the coach was rocketing forwards and Igor was as happy as a sandboy.

'This is the way it should be done,' he said, squashing a parked car which happened to be in his way.

Holding on to the wheel with one hand, Igor began driving back towards the zoo.

Even walking wasn't very easy when you had legs of different lengths. This was something Igor had discovered when he was very young because unless he was very careful he always ended up walking in circles. However, it was only now he realized that his legs made driving difficult as well. He learned this when he eventually found the two vampires. Samuel had been unable to fight the effects of the tranquillizer any longer and was fast asleep under a huge oak tree. Fenella was sitting beside him, wondering how she could get him back to Blood Castle, when Igor clattered towards them in the bus.

'Over here, Igor,' she shouted excitedly, leaping to her feet. 'Stop by the tree.'

This was what Igor would have liked to do but stopping was the problem. Although he knew where the right pedal was, he couldn't quite reach it with his left foot. The only way to stop the coach was to drive it into a tree. It was the same tree Samuel had been sleeping under and the large branch which fell on his head woke him up.

'What's the matter?' he cried, leaping to his feet in alarm. 'Where am I?'

'It's all right, Uncle,' Fenella said, patting him on the shoulder. 'I'm here.'

'So am I, Master.' Igor had climbed unsteadily out of the coach. 'We're going to collect your coffin, then I'm going to drive you home.'

'Drive me home?' Samuel had just noticed the coach. 'In that fiendish human contraption? Never. I'll fly home the way I always do.' Samuel started hopping and prancing around on the grass, flapping his arms as hard as he could.

'We can't fly, Uncle.' Although Fenella didn't want Igor to drive her either, she knew there was no choice. 'The sunlight will ruin our wings.'

'In that case, I'll stay here,' Samuel decided. 'I was perfectly comfortable under the tree until Igor tried to knock it down.'

Samuel was still feeling very sleepy. Although the drug had nearly worn off by now, it was the middle of the day, a time when old vampires should be resting. It wasn't until Fenella told him that the men would lock him in a cage again if he stayed that Samuel finally agreed to board the coach. Even then, however, he didn't want Igor to drive. 'You're a good servant, Igor,' he said, 'but you're not very good with machines. Why, you couldn't even manage something as simple as the SALAD.'

'That was different, Master,' Igor protested. 'Driving a bus is easy. I drove here from the car park all right.'

'What about the tree?' Samuel asked. 'I suppose you hit that on purpose.'

'Yes, Master. It was the only way I could stop. My leg wasn't long enough to reach the stop pedal.'

'Terrific,' Samuel told him. 'Every time we need to stop, you'll have to crash into something. Are Fenella's legs long enough to reach this stop pedal of yours?'

'Yes, Master.'

'In that case she can drive. I'll feel safe with her.'

'But I don't know what to do, Uncle.'

'Igor will explain everything to you, dear. There's no need to worry.'

Before either Fenella or Igor had a chance to argue any more, Samuel settled down on one of the seats and went to sleep.

Madame Romany the Gypsy Fortune-Teller was really Beryl Smith from Manchester and the only caravan she had been inside was near the beach at Blackpool. However, Leticia Crumb didn't know this. It was her first visit to a fortune-teller and she was finding it all very exciting. The tent was dimly lit and she thought Madame Romany looked most impressive in her gypsy robes. So did the large parrot on a perch behind her.

'Can you really see into the future, Madame Romany?' Leticia asked excitedly.

'Of course I can, child. When I gaze into my crystal ball, everything is revealed to me.'

'And does the parrot help?'

'He has his uses,' Madame Romany answered mysteriously.

Mostly the parrot just made a mess on the floor, but the fortune-teller wasn't about to admit this. Waving her hands over the crystal ball on the table in front of her, Madame Romany stared into the glass. 'The mists are beginning to clear,' she began in a deep voice. 'I can see . . . I can see . . . .'

'Yes, what can you see?' Leticia was almost breathless with excitement.

'I see a stranger,' the fortune-teller intoned. 'A tall stranger coming into your life.'

'Yes, yes.' By now Leticia was bouncing up and down on her seat. 'Go on.'

'The stranger is travelling from afar and—'

Madame Romany had no chance to make up any more because at that moment a large coach came careering through the fairground, flattening her tent and knocking both the fortune-teller and Leticia from their seats. It was several seconds before they managed to untangle themselves.

'I do hope my stranger wasn't on that bus,' Leticia said sadly, watching the coach crash through the fence on the far side of the field.

Fenella wasn't stopping for anything and Madame Romany and Leticia weren't the only ones to notice her as she drove along. Walter Bucket, the window cleaner, saw her as she came driving along the pavement, taking his ladder away with her. It was almost an hour before the fire engine came to rescue him from the upstairs windowsill where he was hanging and another day before he could get his arms down by his side again. Bertram Trowel noticed her when she demolished the garden wall he had just finished building. And thirty-seven members of an angling club certainly noticed her when Fenella took a short cut along the towpath where they were fishing. They all had to jump into the canal to avoid being run over.

There were lots of other people as well, but Fenella didn't care because she was enjoying herself. Driving was so much more restful than flying, and she thought she was doing rather well. In fact, she was disappointed that Uncle Samuel had retired to his coffin for a snooze and wasn't there to watch her. Fenella knew she was driving much better than all those silly humans in their little cars. They all followed the road, however much it twisted and turned, while any sensible vampire knew it was much, much quicker to travel in a straight line.

'You're right, Igor,' she said happily, swerving to miss the apple tree in Beatrice Mumble's back garden. 'Driving is easy.'

'Yes, Miss Fenella.' Poor Igor was absolutely terrified. If he had had any hair, it would probably have turned white.

'I think I'm doing jolly well, considering I've never tried before.'

'Yes, Mistress.'

Fenella swerved back on to the road, destroying two telegraph poles and a fence. 'Why do you keep putting your hands over your eyes?' she asked, looking across at Igor again. 'Do you feel ill or something?'

'No, Miss Fenella.'

'Are you sure? You're trembling all over and you're very pale.'

Fenella should have been looking at the road instead of at Igor. If she had, she would have seen the Rolls-Royce which was parked ahead of her. Spiro Pasta had taken a short-cut. He was determined to recapture his vampires and neither of them would escape a second time.

'They're coming, Boss,' Luigi shouted, running back towards the Rolls.

'Right,' Spiro said, grinning his evil smile. 'We've got them.'

As soon as the breathless Luigi had scrambled aboard, Spiro moved the car so it was completely blocking the road. Then he turned to the Lasagna brothers who were sitting in the back seat. 'You two stay where you are until I need you to carry the vampires,' he told them. 'That way I know there won't be any more mistakes.'

'What are you going to do?' Laszlo asked.

'I'm going to put those vampires properly to sleep.' Spiro held up the tranquillizer dart he had taken from his pocket. 'It's extra, extra strength, just like the one that's already in the gun. This dart would put an elephant to sleep for months. We'll have plenty of time to get those vampires back to the zoo and lock them up so they can't possibly escape.'

Spiro climbed out of the car to stand in the road. He could hear the coach approaching the corner. 'Right, Luigi,' he said, putting his hand in the window. 'Give me the gun.'

'What gun, Boss?'

'The tranquillizer gun, idiot. The one which shoots the darts.'

'But I haven't got it, Boss.'

'What do you mean?' Spiro couldn't believe his ears. 'You must have it. How else are we going to capture the vampires?'

'I haven't got it, Boss. Really I haven't. The vampire took it away from me.'

'You could always throw the dart,' Laszlo suggested. 'I'll shout out, "One hundred and eighty," if you hit a vampire.'

Spiro was far too terrified to pay any attention. He was standing in the middle of the road, a coach with two bloodsucking vampires aboard was almost at the corner and he didn't have a weapon to stop them with. As the coach came into sight, Spiro dropped the dart he was holding and dived headfirst into the ditch beside the road.

Although it was a very muddy ditch, it was just as well he did. Fenella was still looking at Igor as the coach came racing round the corner and she didn't even see the car in the middle of the road until she hit it. Cccrrraaassshhh! The coach came to a dead halt while the Rolls-Royce started rolling backwards, gathering speed as it went down the hill. The hill was as steep as the ditch was muddy and there was another corner at the bottom but the Rolls continued straight on, smashing through a farm gate and scattering a herd of cows before it finally came to a halt in the middle of a large haystack. Only then did Fenella turn to look at Igor. His face had gone as white as the dandruff on top of his head.

'What a silly place to leave a motorcar,' she said.

'If I wasn't such a good driver, somebody might have been hurt.'

Igor was far too shaken by the crash to answer. Besides, he was looking at the mud-covered figure which was crawling out of the ditch. There was something familiar about the man. 'That's him, Mistress,' he shouted suddenly.

'That's who, Igor?'

'The man who was in the lorry the day the master was stolen.'

'Are you sure, Igor?'

'Oh yes, Miss Fenella. I'd recognize him anywhere.' Although Igor wasn't very good at reading and counting, he was excellent at remembering faces.

'In that case,' Fenella said grimly, 'he's somebody I've been wanting to meet for some time.'

When Spiro saw Fenella jump angrily from the coach, he decided he wanted to be somewhere else, somewhere a long way away. Unfortunately for him, being rich had made him fat and being fat wasn't very good for running. Spiro only managed a couple of steps before a long arm reached out, grabbed hold of his collar and lifted him from the ground as though he were a feather. 'Where do you think you're going, you horrible little human,' Fenella hissed, her eyes flashing behind the goggles.

'I'm in a hurry,' Spiro squeaked, his legs still

running although he was being held high in the air. 'I've got to see a man about a dog.'

'First of all you've got to see a vampire about her uncle. What do you mean by stealing him and locking him up in a cage?'

'I didn't steal him.' Spiro was blubbering with fear. 'It was Luigi and Laszlo. I didn't have anything to do with it.'

'Oh yes he did, Mistress.' Igor had left the coach to join Fenella. 'He was the man in the lorry all right.'

'What do you have to say to that?' Fenella demanded fiercely.

'I'm sorry,' squeaked Spiro.

'Sorry?' Fenella almost roared the word as she pushed her face close to his. All the terrified Spiro could see was her teeth, teeth which could have ripped him to shreds in seconds. 'Sorry? Is that the best you can manage?'

'I'm very, very, very, very, very sorry indeed,' babbled Spiro. 'Ever so, ever so, ever so sorry and it won't happen again.'

'Too right it won't,' Fenella snarled. 'What's your name, you miserable microbe?'

'Piro Spasta. I mean Sasta Piro.'

'Come on,' Fenella said impatiently. 'Make your mind up.'

'It's Spiro Pasta,' Spiro managed at last.

'Well, Mr Pasta, you'd better listen to me. I know your name and I know where you live.

What's more, I'm going to tell all my friends about you. If anything else happens to my uncle, we'll all come visiting, hundreds and hundreds of us. I'm sure you don't want that to happen.'

As she spoke, Fenella shook Spiro so hard his teeth rattled and his eyes spun round like catherine wheels.

'N-n-n-no I d-d-d-don't,' he stammered.

'Well, make sure it isn't necessary and pass on the message to your friends Yogi and Lilo. I don't want to see any of you ever again.'

Her warning finished, Fenella tossed Spiro back into the ditch he had just crawled out of. She was turning away from him when she noticed Samuel climbing out of the coach, a strange-shaped stick in his hand.

Tired as he had been, Samuel had found it very difficult to sleep with his coffin bouncing around at the back of the coach. Even when the coach stopped, he didn't have much more success. There was something hard digging into his ribs, stopping him from settling comfortably.

'It's not right,' he complained to himself. 'People put me to sleep when I'm feeling wide awake. Then when I'm tired, nobody will let me rest.'

Samuel climbed wearily out of his coffin and fished around inside until he found what had been digging into him. It was the gun he had taken from Luigi in the cage. 'Perhaps I ought to shoot myself with it,' he muttered. 'That way I'd be sure of a decent sleep.'

On the other hand, he would probably wake up feeling strange again and Samuel wasn't so sure this was a good idea. While he was up and about, Samuel decided to go and see why the coach had stopped and he was just in time to see Fenella throw somebody in a ditch. 'Was he a friend of yours?' he asked.

'Certainly not, Uncle. That was one of the men who stole you from the castle. I've just explained what's going to happen to him if he interferes with us again.'

'Good for you, dear.' Samuel was too tired and too hungry to be bothered with silly humans. 'Aren't we nearly home yet?'

'Yes, Master,' Igor told him. 'We'd be able to see the castle if there weren't trees in the way.'

'Jolly good,' Samuel said. 'By the way, what do you think I ought to do with this, dear?'

'What is it, Uncle?' Like Samuel, Fenella had often heard about guns but the one he was hold-ing up to her was the first one she had actually seen.

'It's what those men used to put me to sleep with. It shoots a nasty little dart thing which pricks into you. I think you have to pull this to make it work.'

Making sure the gun wasn't pointing anywhere near Fenella or Igor, Samuel pulled the trigger and the dart shot off into the long grass beside the ditch. 'Interesting, isn't it?'

'I suppose so, Uncle, but it isn't any use to us.'

'You're right, of course.' Samuel dropped the gun in the road. 'Shall we get going? It's so long since I last had anything to eat, I've almost forgotten how to use those False Replacement Teeth you gave me.'

'We'll have to walk, Master.' For some reason, Igor seemed very happy about this. 'The bus is broken.'

The front of the coach had a huge dent in it where it had hit Spiro's car. Even though Fenella and Samuel didn't know anything about human machines, they could see Igor was right. Luckily, Blood Castle wasn't far away and after Fenella had collected the coffin they set off, taking a short cut across the fields. All any of them wanted to do was get home.

They were hardly out of sight when Luigi and Laszlo came running up the road, looking like a couple of moving haystacks. Although it had taken them some time to push the bales of straw out of the way and escape from the car, neither of them were hurt.

'There's no sign of any of them,' Luigi said, looking around.

'Perhaps those vampires have eaten the boss up

and gone off to be sick,' Laszlo suggested. 'Or maybe—'

'Wait a minute,' Luigi interrupted him. 'What's that funny noise?'

For a few seconds they both listened. The noise sounded rather like water gurgling down a plughole and it was coming from the tall grass beside the ditch. 'Go and see what it is, Laszlo.'

'Not likely. It might be a dangerous animal.'

'Don't be so daft. There aren't any around here.'

'Says who? Those vampires seemed pretty dangerous to me.'

There was no saying how long they might have continued arguing if Luigi hadn't suddenly realized what the noise was. It was a sound he had heard many times before when he took Spiro his breakfast in bed. 'It's the boss,' he said excitedly, starting towards the ditch. 'I'd recognize that snore anywhere.'

And Luigi was right. When they looked in the grass, there was a mud-spattered Spiro Pasta, sleeping as peacefully as a baby.

'The vampires didn't eat him after all.' Laszlo sounded rather disappointed.

'No, they shot him instead.' Luigi was pointing at the tranquillizer dart Samuel had shot from the gun. Now it was sticking up from Spiro's bottom. 'How long did he say the dart would put an elephant to sleep for.'

'Months and months.'

'That means the boss will probably be like this for years and years. It's Sleeping Beauty all over again.'

'He looks more like Sleeping Ugly to me,' Laszlo said.

Slowly a big smile spread across Luigi's face. 'Sleeping Ugly,' he said delightedly. 'Laszlo, my boy, I think it's our turn to make a fortune.'

'What do you mean?'

'We can put him in the empty vampire cage with a big sign outside. "The Sleeping Ugly," it'll say. "Wake him up and win a prize." We can charge the visitors a pound each to throw wet sponges and wooden balls and rotten fruit at him.'

'Even if they do hit him, he won't wake up.' By now Laszlo's smile was as wide as his brother's.

'Of course,' Luigi went on, 'the boss isn't going to be very pleased when he does finally wake up.'

'There won't be much he can do about it if he's locked in a cage. Besides, we can always put him back to sleep again.'

Whistling cheerfully, the two Lasagna brothers picked up the snoring Spiro Pasta and started off down the road to the zoo.

'Ish ruly mice tube buck horn,' Samuel said contentedly.

'Teeth, Uncle,' Fenella reminded him. 'You've forgotten them again.'

'I'm sorry, dear.' Samuel quickly removed the teeth from his mouth. 'I was saying it's really nice to be home again.'

'It must be.' Fenella was thinking of her own cosy crypt. It seemed a long time since she had last been there. 'I think I shall have to be leaving soon.'

'Not just yet, dear. There's one thing we have to do first.'

'I know, Master,' Igor broke in. 'You need some more sandwiches.'

'Perhaps a little bit later, Igor. I was thinking of the SALAD. Fenella hasn't seen it working yet.'

'I've just remembered, Master.' Igor had started to edge away from the table. 'There's a lot of washing up to do and I really ought to rearrange the cobwebs in the dungeon.'

He would have scuttled off if Samuel hadn't reached out to grab hold of his arm. 'You can't go, Igor. We need you to test it for us.'

'But I've already tried it once, Master,' Igor said nervously. Being driven in a coach by Fenella had been bad enough but being thrown off the battlements again would be far worse. 'It didn't work.'

'That's only because you aren't very good at counting,' Fenella pointed out. 'This time I'll

count up to three for you. You'll know just when to pull the handle.'

'But—'

'No more, "buts",' Samuel said firmly. 'You're wasting time.' Despite his protests, the two vampires hustled Igor up to the battlements. Before he knew it, the SALAD was strapped to his back and he had been lifted up on to the wall. It looked even further to the ground than it had done previously.

'There's one thing you've forgotten, Master,' Igor said desperately.

'Oh no I haven't. I've checked everything thoroughly.'

'But I still can't . . . .' Nobody was listening. Samuel gave Igor a push in the back and once again he was hurtling down from the battlements.

'One,' Fenella counted out loud, 'two, three, PULL.'

Igor pulled the handle and suddenly he was no longer hurtling towards the ground. A huge canopy in the shape of a bat's wing had blossomed above him and he was drifting gently towards the ground.

'It works, Uncle,' Fenella cried delightedly.

'I always knew it would.'

'Congratulations. You really are a clever old thing.'

Fenella was so busy nuzzling her uncle's neck that she didn't see Igor drift gently into the moat. Nor did Samuel. The first they knew of it was when they heard his startled cries for help.

'You did . . . glub, glub . . . forget,' he bellowed. 'I still . . . glub, glub . . . can't swim . . . glub, glub.'

There were times when being a vampire's servant really wasn't very much fun at all.